Penguin Books

The Banquet

Carolyn Slaughter was born in India and spent much of her childhood in Africa. She now lives in London. *The Banquet* is her sixth novel, the others being *The Story of the Weasel*, which won the Geoffrey Faber Memorial Prize, *Columba*, *Magdalene*, *Dreams of the Kalahari* and *Heart of the River*.

The Banquet confirms Carolyn Slaughter as a 'fine novelist' with 'a magical gift for storytelling' (*New Standard*). The *Irish Times* wrote of her first novel: 'Carolyn Slaughter's sensitivity, originality and breadth of imagination surpass those of many a more seasoned novelist.' Her second book was called 'a stunning, profound and wounding performance' by the *Sunday Times*, and her fourth was described by *The Times* as a 'strong, beautifully controlled novel . . . fierce steely writing across a range of emotions as dangerous as any we may remember'.

The Banquet

Carolyn Slaughter

 Penguin Books

Penguin Books Ltd, Harmondsworth, Middlesex, England
Penguin Books, 40 West 23rd Street, New York, New York 10010, U.S.A.
Penguin Books Australia Ltd, Ringwood, Victoria, Australia
Penguin Books Canada Ltd, 2801 John Street, Markham, Ontario, Canada L3R 1B4
Penguin Books (N.Z.) Ltd, 182–190 Wairau Road, Auckland 10, New Zealand

First published by Allen Lane 1983
Published in Penguin Books 1984

Made and printed in Great Britain by
Cox & Wyman Ltd, Reading
Filmset in 10 on 12 point Monophoto Sabon
by Northumberland Press Ltd, Gateshead

For P.M. and M.G.

'Twas far too strange, and wonderful for sadness;
Sharpening, by degrees, his appetite
To dive into the deepest.

JOHN KEATS

One

I am waiting for them to come. I'm not frightened at all. Their coming for me is the only certainty, so I hold to it. I even want them to come. Once I would have considered this most strange, but not now, because now I'm not the man I have been all the rest of my life. I'm like a man who's been washed up on an unknown island after a violent shipwreck; when the storm and the sea have finished with you, to have survived seems strangely irrelevant.

Yesterday is already a memory, and, as with all memory, you can bring back only those emotions you desire – my lips on her flesh, her flesh on my lips. Our sweat mingling on hot afternoons with the children calling to one another outside and the sudden silence when they were summoned inside.

My heart just stopped. That chair over there, the one like a throne – I can't look at it again – just now when I looked at it, I saw her hat. It was nestling in the purple velvet of the seat. Her hat: a fat crown of golden straw with poppies flopping over the brim. I ache to hold it, smell it, but if one glance can fell me, what would touch do? If I turn my chair I won't be able to see it.

Once the beauty of this room would have comforted me; everything in it was chosen for its perfection. By that I don't mean a perfect symmetry of form, but everything in this room I found so lovely in its way that I had to have it, whatever the cost. But I feel only the Buddha has forgiven me, that he watches me through his great eyes as wisely and kindly as he's always done. The other things in the room are wary of me.

When I first saw her she was touching peaches; her hands moving quickly over the waxed paper in the tray. I watched her as she picked up one of the peaches; she seemed to weigh it in her hand and the luscious flowery smell of the fruit hung as close as a curtain around her. I felt that she wanted to bite into that peach; the pleasure in her face, feeling the weight of it, was so intense it was as though she'd grown it herself.

I was standing behind her and I could see the bent nape of her creamy neck with her blonde curls held up away from it. I had an overpowering impulse to lick her neck. Oh my love, what pain to think of this now. She moved, replacing the peach. I felt it was me she was setting aside. She moved her head, ever so slightly, so what I saw was the barest profile of a face – because no sooner had she turned towards me than she moved away. But in that instant my heart gave way. It stopped. You question this – that a heart stops? But hair grows white at a stroke, I have seen it happen, to my father. He too was a man who lacked the ability to let go. Strange that I should feel myself close to him now when I am most alone.

All I saw of her that day was half of her mouth, the nub of a chin, slope of a pale forehead. But that brief sight filled me with such a sense of imminent joy, of hope, of laughter, that it brought me close to tears. Her ripeness, the intimate smell of her skin mingling with the sleepy smell of those peaches gave me such a blast of pure happiness.

The phone rings. Again. As it rang yesterday. Of course I can't answer it. I have to give myself as much time as I can, to prepare myself for their judgements. I cannot at this moment remember exactly what happened; my mind is shielding me from reality. Mercifully I am aloof from myself still. It will not last. Nor will this time of waiting. Yesterday evening the doorbell rang. I turned to stone and couldn't move for an hour or more. I sat watching the door as if it had acquired life by that harsh ring. But it did not ring again.

Then I worked out how long I have. Until this afternoon, tomorrow at the latest, no longer. By then someone will have informed the police.

Two

His name was Harold Moreton. He was walking quickly down High Street Kensington. It was just after nine in the morning and the streets were doused with sunshine so that the people walking them looked more cheerful than usual. Harold had a small smile on his lips; so content did he look that an elderly woman watching him credited him with a fine digestion. In his face, which was lean and well proportioned, almost handsome, just the inkling of childhood remained, as if he allowed a chink of that door to remain open to give him a sharper vision of the world. He was thirty-one.

The doors of Marks and Spencer were open and he walked in. It was a Thursday and he always went to Marks on Thursdays; he went on Tuesdays too, quite regularly. He walked, more slowly now, down the side of the shop floor. Young shopgirls – sales assistants – were ritually wiping the surfaces around the tills, dusting the racks, straightening and arranging the frocks into sizes. He stopped to listen as one of them said fiercely: 'Of course *she* asked him round to come and fix her car again last night, didn't she? Opened the door wearing only her flamin' knickers and a T-shirt. I told him if it's her body he's fixin' I'll . . .'

A neat voice interjected, 'Miss Morgan, will you go and get some more fourteens in the lambswool, please. See what's left downstairs.'

'Yes, Mrs Lipton.' A schoolgirl had replaced the indignant woman.

Harold smiled at her and walked on. He breathed in happily, he felt so at home in the store. He loved it, he loved to wander through its carefully arranged corridors picking up titbits of the girls' lives. He loved them, the way they talked and laughed, their clean hair and sweet young faces, even their dreadful uniforms. And in this particular Marks and Spencer, his Marks and Spencer, he loved them most particularly because at some point or other in their day they would be close to her, would sit beside her at a table, talk to her in some changing room, walk with her down the stairs to the world outside.

Once he had tried Woolworth's. He'd stood waiting in a queue; two girls were lounging on the till – a tall one talking non-stop to the other who was painting her nails with her mouth slightly ajar. They weren't bothering with the queue of customers. Finally the tall girl sighed and stopped talking; her friend's nails had dried, though she shook and blew at them from time to time. Then she snatched at the first customer's purchase, stuffed it into a bag, cursed because it nicked her nail, and snarled out the price as if the customer was taking a great liberty in making a purchase in the first place. Harold never went to Woolworth's again.

Now he was walking more briskly past Coats and Ladies' Trousers and was making for the Food Hall. His step slowed visibly and his confidence seemed to leave him. He picked up a wire basket and walked slowly towards the wine, put two bottles of Beaujolais in his basket and walked over to the fruit and vegetables. She was nowhere to be seen. His heart tumbled. She was always here at this time. He chose some apples and grapefruit, then began to search the area behind him again. Turning the corner to get some onions and asparagus, he saw her.

She was standing on a small stepladder near the cold-storage display. She was counting, calling down figures to a dark girl who was standing below her. She almost lost her balance on the steps and laughed: he felt himself go quite still with pleasure.

A woman pushed at him to get to the oranges and he woke. He moved closer to the stepladder and pretended to look among the ham and bacon. Her long legs seemed to be dusted with a pale shimmering sheen, and beneath her blue pinafore white lace flickered briefly each time she stretched. When she stretched a soft curve became swollen in her thigh. The plain uniform could not hide the long sweep of her thighs, the hard buttocks rushing into her waist. She turned to come down, putting her hand out momentarily to the dark girl to steady herself. Harold steadied himself by taking three deep breaths.

It was her face. Her mouth. It must be the most beautiful and exotic mouth in the world, unique and quite extraordinary. She had not one but two perfectly etched cupid's bows – one on the top lip, the other, remarkably, on the bottom lip. It was as if she had two top lips, one on top of the other, kissing each other. Desire gripped him so hard that he felt faint. Vaguely he heard her say, 'If there isn't enough, ring down to Fran. Make sure you fill all the rows.' She was walking towards him; he could see the blue plastic badge with an M & S above it and her name, Miss B. Bailey, moulded into it. Her face was turned away from him as she walked towards the check-out counter. He stood there, watching her go.

He had begun to sweat and his breathing was quick and low, but he didn't follow her. He began to study the label announcing the origin of the bunch of grapes. He was remembering the time when he had come and she really had been gone. How he had frantically searched the Food Hall until anxiety had compelled him to ask for her. His turmoil was so profound – imagining her ill or gone altogether – that he could barely take in the helpful voice of the girl who replied, 'Oh, she's not on Foods today, she's covering on Plants. We're short of Deps today.' She went on tapping out the buttons on the till like morse code even as she gave him the information. He was so grateful that she had to call him back for his change. There was something about her directness and simplicity that made him feel overbred.

Plants. He had walked towards it but stood a little way off. She was standing like a pale lily in a green forest. By the glossy greenery of their foliage, the ferns and weeping figs set off her skin surrounded by its sunburst of blonde hair. She had just finished talking to a customer and seemed to stop and catch her breath. He was drawn forward, his heart beating violently with relief. For the next ten minutes he pretended to look at the silk scarves and it pleasured him to feel their texture while watching her. Ten minutes was all he would allow himself before moving off; he never looked back at her.

For two months, religiously, every Tuesday and Thursday, he'd gone to the store to look at her. It was a little like the visits he used to make to the V. & A. to look at the exquisite encased objects, things impossible to touch or feel, behind glass, quite inaccessible. Sometimes a lust to hold a vase or a plate would cramp his insides. It was the same with her. But by now he knew that it was more than a lust for possession. He'd never known it was possible – so much feeling, so great a tenderness – it was like an explosion of love within him. But he knew the power and destruction of love, so he held back from her, waiting, until he was quite certain.

Three

I had become obsessed then in a way that I'd never been before and in a way that I know I will never be again. Some women mark you: she left me with a deep wound in my emotional tissue. It is so physical that I can feel it throbbing. And after the throbbing, which is like the skin tearing on a burn, when that has passed, something in me will have died. That place will never feel again; it has been cauterized.

Watching her was most extraordinary. She seemed to affect every one of my senses. She stood there, totally absorbed in her work, unaware of me as I watched her. That full supple body, the bloom of her skin ... but at the same time I could hear her voice (she hummed to herself a lot) and when I drew closer my nose quivered at the unadorned scent of her. This last sense was the strongest – until I first touched her. But that was much later. In those early months I only watched her obsessively, all of me straining, reaching an unbearable pitch of excitement and desire and fear.

One day I came in determined to find which part of her was flawed and which part of her she liked least. We all have something about our bodies that we try to hide (it's why I wear gloves so much; my hands don't seem part of me, they're too much like my father's hands, blunt and insensitive). But if she had some small secret dislike, I never discovered it. Even when I knew every corner of her most intimately I could never find a part of her that she disliked. She moaned about her hair or her nails when they broke, but no part of her was marred, no part of her was secret.

I keep wondering if I'd ever been obsessed before, in any way. There was Rachel of course, but she was a thorn in the flesh; with her there was no bud, no blooming, just a withering of hope and feeling. But there was a young girl, long ago, an American girl. I thought of her with a kind of madness and watched her from a tortured distance. She had long, long hair the colour of ripe apricots. But an obsession? It's so hard to say.

I was seventeen, quite innocent and as revolting as most boys of that age, I suppose. She was fifteen – perhaps. I saw her on a beach near Arcachon where my father and I spent a number of holidays together. She is all I remember of those strained weeks my father and I spent in one another's company. I followed her and she tossed me quick arrogant glances as she walked home and then disappeared into a stone house, square and elegant with wonderful gardens.

She was a most sophisticated American – she wouldn't have recognized a hamburger or a wash 'n' wear garment; she was brought up to be European. She spoke immaculate French, wore beautifully cut clothes and held her knife and fork the right way. She was staying with her cousins for the month of August and she talked loudly to them as they all ran down the beach to the water. My vocabulary consisted mainly of *pardon, je m'excuse* and *merci* – all mumbled into my shoulder to disguise my awful accent. I was completely graceless, gauche and skinny as only an English boy can be.

The American girl was haughty and capricious. She danced on the empty beach in the late evening light. She knew that I watched her, but she did her poised ballet steps entirely for herself, depriving me. She would saunter past me, and if I let her see me she would give a little sneer – what an intoxication that was! She drove me to distraction with that and her mocking laugh. Once I stumbled and almost fell at her feet – when I think about her majestic disdain, I'm amazed at my persistence. And how marvellous the way she looked down at me half-sprawled at her feet, and with casual disregard, mimicking my accent, said, 'Oh, bad luck.' A superb bitch. I can even enjoy her now – but then – what agonies.

Perhaps that kind of obsession is the most delicious suffering and that's what we miss when it's ended. I remember that on the evening I was first granted entry into the American girl's house I felt she had asked me so that she could torment me more easily. It was one of those French country houses full of light falling on dark gleaming furniture, bowls of peaches and tall vases of gladioli and irises. We all sat around the table for dinner: cousins and friends, people of all ages. The long table was crammed with superb food (perhaps that was the beginning of my gourmet days?) and decanters of expensive wine. Everyone talked around me; they took little notice of me because of my infirmity: I still hadn't mastered their language. While they ate I felt I was dying. Because, although she had asked me to come, she wasn't there. It got late and I so much forgot myself that I began surreptitiously to gnaw my nails, which was a habit I hated most and never did in public. I began to grow sick with disappointment.

An extraordinary moment! In the soft lamplight suddenly she appeared. She seemed to float in and stood there just inside the door of the large dining room. She had danced in and stood there, one arm stretched in front of her, her back arched, her right leg slowly, slowly raising itself to the level of her shoulder. We all watched her in silence as she stood, poised and beautiful, wearing only a white nightdress so that on her slim frame her breasts looked large and full and very sharply visible.

Her aunt made an odd noise which sounded half like a gasp and half like a slap. A ripple of discontent arose. She held her pose for another moment and then seemed to crack with a harsh movement as her body returned to that of a normal mortal. She looked at her aunt viciously and ran from the room.

I followed her and I only had the courage to do it because I had divined some suffering in her; she was vulnerable at last and I knew I could comfort her. It was the only trait I could put my trust in: my ability to be sympathetic. At school people always told me their secrets. I found her at the beach; she saw me but ignored me. I sat beside her silently, I could see she had been crying hard. I didn't touch her; she was the ideal of purity and beauty to me, touch was unthinkable.

She got up swiftly and I was prepared to let her go. But to my amazement she turned and jerked her head at me in an eloquent signal to follow her into the dark pine undergrowth.

In there she taught me all that her uncle had taught her. But what she taught me was so full of her anger and suffering that it hurt me as it had hurt her. Afterwards the episode sickened me.

There is nothing of that in what I feel about you, my love, there's nothing but love left in me now.

Four

Strange to remember the American girl – if that was obsession, then there's no comparison with what I felt for Blossom. With Blossom there was great happiness. And she loved me. It is these two things that I must hold to.

In the beginning I was perfectly happy just to follow her as she walked around the Food Hall, talking to the girls and the customers, checking lists, opening up new tills. I grew to know her in my head. I became familiar with all her movements: her sniff, her way of sliding her finger under her nose, how she would twist a particular curl behind her left ear. I began to invent a life for her away from the store – with a mum and dad, a brother perhaps, but no sexual entanglements. I became certain that she was free and that no man had really touched her. Very slowly she grew to be mine – she was that familiar and she became that dear to me. When I say *mine* I mean it in an absurd fantastic way, of course; what I really mean is I began to feel that she was the woman I had waited and saved myself for all those lonely years.

I began to hate to leave her. Walking out of that store and going home, the nights following the days that I saw her, those were the bleakest times of my life. Perhaps that's why I didn't go more often – the toll was too high. I hadn't the courage to approach her. I'm not even sure I wanted to. It was so perfect the way things were between us. And I knew she could cause me great damage – somehow, all my great happiness in her, even then, had a sense of foreboding. Perhaps this attracted me. It was one of the things that drew me once to Buddhism – that belief that all happiness is tinged with its inevitable decay.

In my longing for her I took to walking the streets again.

I had done it when I first came to London and was terribly lonely. There had been a desperate, even a furious quality to my walking as a student; I could keep it up all night, often I did. I saw some very strange things and people told me very strange things at that desolate time between two in the morning and dawn; it was when I really learnt the art of listening to other people's sorrows – and saw how it could comfort me too

Now when I walked the night I did it very slowly, hour after hour observing the light behind windows, catching sight of paintings or vases of flowers; a woman and a baby playing on a cream carpet. In the early evenings I often returned to this window – it was in an old house with a lot of heavy creeper on the walls, like my own childhood house. The windows were small and narrow – it was along the Embankment – and I stood in the shadows and watched the woman playing with the baby on a pink sofa in a softly lit room with bowls of anemones and a big straw basket full of toys.

Often, coming back from these walks, I felt a heaviness in me, but I knew it was not a sadness, more an accumulation of emotion which was growing heavier as my needs grew. But still I waited – for there is a perfect moment in life if you can just capture it, a moment when life is poised in such a way, when you are prepared in such a way, that nothing can disappoint you.

I was waiting for just that moment with her.

Five

One night, after walking a long way from home, he had an extraordinary sense of her presence, as if she were close at hand, in one of the houses that he walked past. The feeling grew so troubling that it forced him to enter a pub, something that he very seldom did, or not since his student days. He did it almost against his will, because he didn't want to be near people, but that night his silent trapped isolation was worse. Once inside the bright pub, his sense of her left him and he felt quite desolate without it.

He decided to stay and sat quietly in a corner drinking whisky, watching people. And, as had happened on his early morning walks, people began to approach him: a man on his own and then a couple tired of one another. They were drawn to him for some reason and would sit down and talk. And he listened. He had a gift for it. He spoke very little himself, but there was something about his way of listening that was gentle and sympathetic. They felt he understood; in fact his quietness, with just an occasional nod of agreement from him, seemed to have a wisdom about it. And he had a smile, a very grave but knowing smile, that had great reassurance in it.

The evening eased him. He knew he would do it again, but in another pub. He knew if he went back, as he was pressed to, a mutual exchange would have to follow, and he didn't want that. It was as if he nursed his solitariness like an old wound, held it jealously to him. For what he wanted was not many people, not a number of loose friendships, but one irrevocable bond, one final connection.

He walked home, it was very late. He went into his sitting room and switched on his stereo set. He put on a David Bowie record and sat down in his chair to listen to it. The wild and wonderful music filled the room. He turned the volume higher and carefully adjusted the controls; louder and louder the volume rose until it seemed to fill not only his body but his brain and heart. But his body did not vibrate at all to the melody although he was quite consumed by the music. He began to feel that his entire being was in a state of unbearable anticipation and that if he were touched, if she would just touch him, he would explode. He knew that his loneliness was poisoning him; that he'd reached a point in his life where he must give up everything in himself, risk everything in himself, submit totally to some human feeling, to some warmth and goodness, to love – or be lost for ever in the past.

The music stopped. Slowly he came back to earth. He looked around his room at all his beautiful possessions, his books, the treasures that made him feel safe. There was a soft light playing on the things that he loved: the oak settle with its delicate carvings, a rosewood table that gleamed with a silvery glow, a rosecoloured glass lamp on the wall, the bowl of lilies on the bureau. There was something very precise about his arrangement of things, something very deliberate and yet absolutely in harmony. It was all very tidy, but it wasn't a feminine tidiness, more the look of things ranged on a desk or of an artist's tools, exactly placed. His room was not a place he merely lived in – it was his entire world.

Now he decided that his house was not a castle, more a fort. No one entered it but the cleaning lady. And he often thought of getting rid of her. But she was a small Spanish woman who usually came when he was out and left notes of her requirements when the wax polish or the Ajax ran out. He never brought anyone to his house if he could help it.

Now he looked about him with a sudden new interest. His house, his shelter – he must prepare it for her. He must try to look at it as she might. He must get it ready for her when she came here. Because she would. She would look so beautiful here. How the room with all its antiques and beauties would become her! She was made to be surrounded by unique and exquisite things. Immediately he got up again and left the house.

He walked briskly up Kensington Church Street to an antique shop he'd passed earlier on and where he had seen a chair in the window: a chair like a throne with a tall stately back and a carved headpiece of mahogany flowers. The seat was upholstered in deep purple velvet and the chair had delicate curved feet. It was perfect. It was made for her. He would buy it for her tomorrow. He grew very excited at the idea. He might never tell her that he'd bought it for her, but it would be hers all the same. Her chair. In his house. Slowly, very slowly, they were getting closer.

Six

The next day was a Friday and he was to lunch with Julian, as always. Before going to the restaurant he'd taken a trip to Knightsbridge to buy himself some new clothes. He hated buying clothes for himself and he had a reluctance towards wearing anything new. He liked what he'd been intimate with for a long time: shirts soft from lots of washing, tweed coats when they'd become mellow, shoes well broken in and shaped exactly to his feet. His clothes were never shabby though, because they had always been very expensive in the first place. But the time had come to invest in a few new clothes; it was part of his preparation for her. He also had his hair cut.

Then he drove to Notting Hill Gate to meet Julian. He was early, so he parked a little way off and walked the distance to the Italian restaurant. As he walked he watched people – quite intently at times. And people who caught his eye would smile at him – he had that sort of face: kind and interested. He was always looking for something extraordinary in everyone he looked at, however ordinary they might appear: the man sweeping the streets, the shopgirl tired and bored – he could always find one aspect of them that was quite perfect. It was what made life wonderful to him: that there was beauty in everything and everyone if you looked for it.

When he got to the restaurant Julian was already sitting in a corner. He looked up and waved when he saw Harold. The waiter greeted Harold warmly and escorted him to the table.

'I was a bit early,' Julian said, 'and I've started on the wine because we have something to celebrate.'

'Have we?' Harold said, sitting down and looking over at the only person he saw on a regular basis, very regularly: once a fortnight, never more, never less.

Julian leaned forward and poured some Frascati into Harold's glass and then beamed. 'Miriam's having a baby,' he announced.

Harold was a little startled but pulled himself into the right attitude quickly. 'Well, congratulations,' he said, 'that's marvellous, marvellous.' Because, after all, what else could you say to someone who was having a baby? But then a curious feeling of, perhaps not envy, but something close to deprivation hit him.

After they had discussed the baby a little, and then work, Julian slid around, as he always did over coffee, to the subject of Harold's private life. It was like a challenge every time he saw Harold to try and get him to talk about this. Even though Julian had worked with Harold in the same architect's office when they were younger, and had known him for years, he still couldn't say that he knew him, or knew anything about the women in Harold's life. But he knew there were women. He'd once seen Harold with a striking dark girl in the park, not so long ago.

He stirred his coffee. 'Remember that girl I saw you with in the park?'

Harold nodded vaguely and looked around for the waiter.

'What was her name?'

'Rachel,' Harold said quietly.

'Still about, is she?' Julian had long ago decided that discreet questions got him nowhere.

Harold smiled his small secret smile. 'Well, no, she's not actually,' he said.

'Hm, seemed a nice girl, very good-looking.'

'It was cold that day,' Harold said absent-mindedly.

'What day?' Julian's eyebrows seemed to wriggle into long lines on his wide forehead.

'That day you saw us in the park. I remember how cold it was.'

'Was it?'

'Yes it was.'

Oh no, thought Julian, he's not going to get me that way, this time I'm going to persevere.

'Anyone else at the moment then?'

'Anyone else what?'

'That you're, well, interested in.'

'Not really. Want a brandy?'

'No thanks – oh yes, well, I might as well.'

It had ended as it always did – no way to get under the surface of that calm exterior. Harold maintained a distance and a secrecy which made it impossible to get close to him. He wouldn't talk about women or his family, or only when questioned and then very briefly. But Julian had always liked him for his quirky sense of humour and his generosity, even though his closeness was infuriating. It always made you feel he had something to hide. Harold had such a subtle way of responding to cross-examinations about his private life that he left people bewildered, but reluctant to continue. You never knew in the end whether he was having a right old time with five fancy women tucked away somewhere, whether he was very discreetly keeping a mistress or whether he was lonely and unwilling to admit it. The evasiveness, which was done so lightly, and accompanied by the small mocking smile, left men feeling curiously envious of him and women intrigued. He was more confusing because he was clearly a man of some sensuality and tenderness and yet he always appeared to be alone.

Harold would say that he loved women, all women, thought they were marvellous, quite marvellous. He believed absolutely in feminism and thought women on the whole far superior to men. It was just that he wouldn't discuss any particular woman. And he tended not to pursue them either. His involvements with women had always come about at their instigation. He was taken up by one of them and would accept the situation and the way it developed without doing much about it himself. Once involved, he was remarkably flexible within a relationship, never making demands or becoming possessive, always behaving with the greatest consideration. Frail women chose him on the whole, those with problems, and he looked after them very well. He often thought of himself as a caretaker, it was his role, always had been, from the days of his mother.

But Rachel had been rather different – she had chosen him all right, but her aggression and his passivity had brought out the worst in both their natures. Once it had ended he refused to see her again. She sometimes rang, making it clear that she wanted to come back to him. It was at this point that his gentleness ended and he became quite hard; once injured there was no return.

The girl in Marks and Spencer was the only woman in his life that he had chosen himself. And because of this it was only natural that she'd been chosen with such great care – and yet at the same time completely spontaneously. And by now he had become aware that she had noticed him; that she even looked at him with a slow sexual expectation. He had spoken to her at last, a breathless moment. And after she'd answered his question she had sort of waited, but he couldn't continue and so she'd walked off with a smile.

Harold picked up the bill firmly. 'No, I'll do it, Julian. After all, you've got all the responsibilities.'

Julian smiled but felt rather lumbered by the idea of the baby, not that Harold would ever have meant the remark in that way. As if to reinforce this he said, 'I'll look around and see if I can find some wonderful cradle or chair for it, or a silver spoon to put in his mouth.'

'I thought I'd ask you to be godfather,' Julian said casually.

'Me?' Harold's face was incredulous.

'Yes, you, why not?'

'Well, I don't think ... religiously, you know, I've fallen by the wayside.'

'To hell with that. I'd like it, really.'

'Well so would I then,' Harold said, 'thank you, Julian.' There was an embarrassed pleasure in him that touched Julian.

After they parted, Harold walked back to his car feeling rather chuffed. He'd send Miriam some flowers and perhaps even accept a dinner invitation, though she was an appalling cook by his standards.

He then decided that he'd buy the throne chair on Saturday morning. He'd mow the lawn and do some gardening on Sunday and then on Tuesday morning he'd go to Marks and Spencer and approach her. He was ready, the moment was upon him, was upon them both. He wondered if she knew it too.

Seven

Today there was something restless about her; he knew it. Today she was vulnerable. He thought how strange it was that her face was never the same, her skin never even the same colour. She had that blondness that takes up tone from everything around it. She was walking quickly around the displays holding a sheaf of paper, but she kept stopping and looking distractedly into space. The skin around her eyes seemed bruised by the night; he wondered if she was unhappy and hesitated.

But he couldn't wait any longer, it would have to be today. She had stopped. So he walked round in front of her and she smiled. Her teeth were thin and pearly as a child's – he wanted to tap a silver knife along them to hear them tinkle.

'Can I help you?'

His voice sounded brisk and low. 'Um, I was looking for the artichokes, I can't seem to find them.' He gave a helpless shrug.

She smiled again, 'I'll check for you.'

He followed her, listening as her heels clicked ahead of him. She led him to the display; a huge mound of artichokes grinned mockingly at him. His hand lifted in a gesture of embarrassment, 'I'm so sorry, I must've walked right past them.'

He thought she would stride off efficiently, but she didn't. He looked at her carefully; her skin that day was the colour of Normandy butter, her mouth was a pale pink, unpolished. She was so clean that he wanted to rumple her; he had an image of her with her head thrown back in ecstasy.

She let her head fall a little. 'Was there anything else you wanted?'

Now he was quite certain; there was something receptive

about her today – not flirtatious, but expectant. He felt like a diver about to plunge into icy water from a rock. He drew himself up, steadied his voice and said with a smile, 'I'd like it very much if you'd come for a walk with me.'

His voice was so gentle and encouraging that her face softened with amusement. A little laugh sneaked out of the corners of her mouth and she tried to pull it back. She looked straight up at him. 'When?' she asked directly. For she too had been watching him – not as long, not as obsessively, but she had seen him, had marked him from the first time he had spoken to her.

'Tonight? Can you? Or perhaps – well, any time that you can?' In his nervousness he began to pull at his fingers.

'After I get off, you mean?' Now it was the friendly voice she used on all her customers.

'Yes.'

'I'm off at six-fifteen tonight.' But she hesitated, remembering that her locker only had the old jeans she'd worn to work. His clothes – a pale blue shirt and tapered jeans with a leather belt – looked carefully chosen and expensive. She'd never seen him in a suit. She wondered what he did, she even wondered if he was out of work – but he was dressed too well, and he certainly ate too well. She'd never seen him buy anything that was frozen.

'Tomorrow would be better,' she said quickly. 'I stop at six.' She found it odd, the suggestion of a walk, not a drink. Had he said a drink, she could have suggested they go to the pub where all the girls went and she'd have felt safer. There was something about him that bothered her, even frightened her a little. His age perhaps, or that he might be married. Though he did his own shopping, so that was unlikely. His eyes were so sharply bright, so watchful.

To cover his disappointment he said, 'Fine, I'll wait outside for you then.' His eyes softened, and his expression, which was normally grave, became open and vivacious.

'And your name, what does the B stand for?' he asked,

indicating the badge. He'd been through the horrible list: Bridget, Brenda, Betty, Bertha, Beryl . . .

'Blossom,' she said, and smiled shyly.

'Blossom!' His face shone with pleasure.

'It was my mum's idea, I was born in the spring, April actually.'

'It suits you.' He wondered what would have happened if she'd turned out black-haired and ugly. 'Your mother must have known you were going to be a beauty.' His voice was low and sensual but she answered brightly, 'Oh, she was lucky.' She said it as though her beauty had nothing to do with her, but was a tribute to her mother's good judgement in selecting her name.

'My name is Harold,' he said, 'Harold Moreton.'

'Oh,' she said quietly, and rubbed her hand under her nose. Then, 'O.K., Harold, tomorrow then,' she said briskly, preparing to go. 'I'll be outside a bit after six because I have to change first.'

'Yes, of course, whenever you're ready. I live just around the corner,' he added.

'See you then, bye.' She turned blithely and walked off.

The joy in him made it impossible to leave, or to take his eyes off her. Her hair was not pulled up off her face today; it hung in a golden cloud about her head, rich and curly. He missed not seeing her neck and the way the little curls fizzled into coils against her skin. And it was her skin, he decided in her absence, that made her so gorgeous – her complexion was flawless, absolutely natural. He felt if he bit into it it would have a sharp sweetness like a nectarine. His mouth watered. She had that perfection of beauty so rare and so touching in a woman of barely twenty.

He walked quickly away, all his nerves tingling, his body in an uproar. 'Blossom,' he whispered, 'Blossom.'

Eight

Blossom got herself a cup of coffee and looked around for a table. She walked over to one close to the lounge area, where there was carpeting, morning papers, and where a young man and his radio sat entwined in a corner. She smiled at the girl already at the table and sat down. There was a fairly clearly defined hierarchy about where to sit in the dining area and really she should sit with the Deputy Supervisors, who sat together, as did the Supervisors. But Blossom wanted to sit on her own and the girl at the table had nearly finished her tea.

Blossom went back to the self-service counter and took a roll, butter, a hunk of cheddar and some marmalade. When she was sitting down again, she cut her roll in half in an abstracted way and began to layer it with butter, cheese and marmalade. She didn't notice the well-built girl who was making her way to her table until she was knocked on the arm.

'Hello Bloss,' Bev said as she plonked herself down in the next chair. 'You on second dinner then?'

'Yeh.'

Bev's dark hair had just been cut into a neat shape around her strongly boned face. She had round cheeks and skin the colour of a gypsy's. Her body was full: it looked as though someone had packed it very tightly, leaving no loose places; it felt very hard to the touch and her hips were wide and solid.

'I like your hair,' Blossom said, admiring the thick straight-ness of it, like a newly clipped privet. 'Have it done this morning?'

'Yeh, not bad is it?' She stirred her tea. 'Don't s'pose Terry'll like it short, say it looks like a fella's.' She felt the back of her neck gingerly.

'It's lovely, Bev, don't mind him, what's he know anyway?'

She was thinking that the Brute, as she called Terry, never looked above Bev's boobs anyway.

Bev said, 'Give us a voucher,' as she stood up, 'I've gone and left mine in my locker and I'm famished.'

She returned with a roll and a currant bun and lots of strawberry jam.

'You coming down to the club tonight, Bloss?' She sawed the roll in half and buttered it. Blossom shook her head.

'You ought to. What's the point of leaving home and us sharing that budgie cage when you don't go out.' She tucked into her currant bun. The funny thing about Blossom, she thought, was that she didn't seem to be looking for anyone; she was waiting for things to come to her. Bev reckoned they never did, unless you got them by the short and curlies.

'I'm going home tonight. Help my mum with the baby. She needs a break.'

'Oh that's all right then, just so's you aren't lonely. Pass us your spoon will you?' She stirred her cup of tea vigorously.

'You going out tonight then, Bev?'

'Yeh, but I tell you, if he goes chatting up that flashy little tart again I'm going to walk out.'

'You know he will,' Blossom said calmly, looking up at the clock.

Bev shook her head and the cropped hair shifted as if it was all one piece, 'No, we had it out. And I told him,' she swallowed the tea too quickly and scalded her tongue, 'bloody hell, that was hot – I told him if he wants to go out with me then he's got to spend the whole bloody evening with me.'

Blossom smiled at her patiently, 'You have to accept the Brute the way he is, or pack it in – he isn't going to get any better. Why'd you stick with him anyway?' She thought of Harold with a sudden pang – but decided not to talk about him. Then she realized how difficult that would be anyway.

Bev wiped her hands on the paper napkin softly and said with a dopey smile, 'Ah, he's lovely really.'

'Oh yeh?' Blossom said in a sarcastic voice, remembering the odd bruise.

Bev leaned forward so that her large jutting breasts rested on the table, 'Well, if you must know, it's really because he says I'm the only one he's had who likes it five times a night.'

Blossom laughed and gave Bev a quick whack on the arm. This was one of the things she liked about Bev; she wasn't clutching on to her virginity until she could trade up for it – not for her the engagement ring, followed by the wedding, the baby, the boredom. Bev was rare amongst the girls they knew, and Bev was bold. Bev, to quote Bev, was after 'a bloody good time and a bloody good fuck'. Trouble was, Blossom thought, she didn't seem to be getting either.

A girl, tiny enough to be one of those Russian gymnasts whose growth has been stunted, joined them. She clonked down her cup and said with hurried curiosity, 'Hey, who was that geyser you were talking to, Blossom?'

'When?' Blossom consulted the clock again.

'You know, earlier. Nice-looking bloke, often comes in, you know the one – the one who's got the hots for you.'

'Oh him,' Blossom said quietly, and Bev noticed that with the nonchalance there was a slight defensive note. The two girls looked at her expectantly so she was forced to add, 'He couldn't find the artichokes.' She could feel to her annoyance that she was blushing.

'Hah,' Bev laughed like a schoolboy, 'and I bet you found them for him, didn't you?'

'Course I did,' Blossom said coolly, standing up. 'Got to go, set a good example and all that.'

'I've still got three minutes. O.K. then Bloss, see you later then. D'you fancy going to Boots at dinnertime? I've got to get some more blusher.'

'Yeh, O.K. Bye.'

Blossom walked past the telephone kiosk at the top of the stairs and hesitated. She wanted to ring her mum, but hadn't got time to go back and get the money from her locker. And suddenly, thinking about her mother working in the launder-ette, as she would be doing now, made Blossom shudder. She could hear the clank of those heavy dryers, smell the steamy stink of old sweat in the clothes as they tumbled about, feel the damp heat of the green-walled room her mum tried so hard to keep clean. But she pulled herself up sharply, reminding herself that anyone who had a job should be grateful. Her dad was a typewriter salesman and had been made redundant – he'd been out of work for eighteen months. It hurt her to think of him.

As she walked down the stairs, she thought instead of the time when he'd been a bus conductor, when she was about four. Those had been the happiest years of a childhood hedged in with hugs and kisses and loving approval. Once she'd ridden on the bus with him when her mum was ill. All the way from Hounslow and back again – it was like driving round the world. She sat on the long seat or on a box in the luggage compartment. It was Christmas time, people were weighed down by parcels and they smiled at her as she sat there, swinging her plump legs. She remembered how her dad kept the bus merry, like an entertainer: he juggled a smile out of a crochety lady, made the shovers wait their turn, rolled out the tickets like long white tongues and produced pennies from the ears of truculent little boys. Her dad's regular audience had said that day how beautiful his little girl was, her golden hair in soft round curls like soap bubbles, her eyes the colour of cornflowers. She laughed as much as her dad did; she could make the cold go out of even those who'd waited twenty minutes for the bus to come along. She was so full of life she couldn't keep still, she couldn't stop laughing, and when the bus emptied a little she began to sing Christmas carols in a high sweet voice.

'Hello Blossom, you going to Dawn's engagement party on Saturday?'

'Oh hello Stella.' Blossom had been walking across the Children's Department on her way down to the ground floor, and she stopped and smiled now, a little vaguely, at a Supervisor with a lovely face, dark caramel in colour, her hair in a multitude of delicate plaits tied back at the crown, each plait tightly bound with gold threads.

'Don't know yet, might have to go home I think.'

They walked across the floor a little as Stella said, 'Hope you can. Have you seen her ring, it's lovely.'

'Hm, how's your baby, Stella?'

'Beautiful.' She rolled the word around in her mouth like a toffee. 'Fat and happy, nearly six months now.'

'And your boyfriend?'

'He's O.K. Getting a car, old one, but nice colour, yellow.'

Blossom touched her arm briefly as they parted, 'See you at dinner maybe. You on second?'

'No, first.'

'Tomorrow then. See you.'

As she walked through the lines of nightdresses and petticoats, Blossom decided she'd buy a big piece of meat for her parents and take it home that night. Best thing to do was to say she'd got it off Waste – the food that was not perfect enough for Marks to sell. It was a lie she often told because in fact the meat was always gone by the time she got down to Waste. Her mum would be pleased as long as she didn't think it was an extravagance. She remembered how as a small girl she'd dreamt of stealing jewels from a department store to give to her mum. Her mum loved pretty things. She couldn't even take her flowers or she'd get: 'I don't want you wasting your money on me, girlie, you've got enough things to spend your wages on.' They wouldn't take a penny off her, now that she'd left home. That made her feel guilty about leaving, when at least before she could contribute to the household expenses; but it had been impossible in the cramped council flat once her sister came back with the baby.

At least her mum was grateful that Blossom got a good lunch – three courses – and all for 10p. It was ridiculous, she said, 10p – you couldn't get a bar of chocolate for that these days. They were very proud of her job, especially since she'd been made up: a Deputy Supervisor at twenty wasn't at all bad. Blossom's mum could boast to her regulars at the launderette: 'My gel can get her hair done, get her feet done, even see the doctor, all at her job, at Marks and Spencer.' They were wonderful people, really you felt she was being looked after as good as at home. You felt she couldn't come to any harm working at a store like that.

The morning drew on slowly. Blossom swapped round the girls at the tills, sent one home when she found her sobbing all over the asparagus because her boyfriend had come off his motorbike, and spent half an hour talking to a woman about her rheumatism. The customers loved her and this made her happy; she always had time for lonely women who used the store in the same way as their family doctor – to air their grievances and glean a little sympathy. Whatever section she was responsible for was immaculate; she wouldn't stand for any careless or rude behaviour towards a customer, not even on Fridays when they were rushed off their feet and sometimes the customers got impatient or bloody-minded. She knew which department brought in the most money in the store. She knew that people were only loyal if you were polite to them and never sold them anything that was off. She wanted to know everything that the store could teach her, to replace her blue pinafore with a Supervisor's uniform, and then look for a job in a posh dress shop. Her ambition was to have a boutique of her own. She was smart enough. It had taken her only a month or two to understand the Marks and Spencer method. But it didn't allow for initiative or drive; you had to do everything their way, you never questioned anything, you did what you were told, and it seemed to her that all the management ended up exactly the same. As Bev said, given half a chance they'd even tell you when you were allowed to fart.

As she walked past the artichokes, Blossom stopped and thought of Harold. On the floor was a crumpled piece of blue paper which she stooped to pick up. She unfolded it to see bold black handwriting on paper with tiny squares all over it. It was a shopping list. She shuddered a little as she read at the bottom of the list, like an item of food, her name – Miss B. Bailey.

Nine

Harold was standing by the door furthest from where the Marks and Spencer girls spilled out into the early evening light, some still in their cream polyester dresses, others changed, chattering like birds freed from a cage. He had placed himself carefully so he could see Blossom before she saw him. He'd grown used to just looking at her and he needed this vantage point to calm himself before approaching her.

A 28 bus came by and carried off some of the girls; the others had dispersed, so that the High Street seemed empty, the pavement outside the doors strangely quiet. It was after six o'clock. Another wave of girls came out; his eyes moved restlessly over them. A moment later she came out of the door by herself. She stood quite still a moment, looking about her with her eyes but barely moving her head. He moved closer to the cover of the wall so that she would not see him. Her hair billowed around her head and shoulders in a profusion of curls. He realized that she had the hair of a very small child, it went with those waxy doll-faces and blue eyes of three-year-olds. But her hair had none of that frizziness, that matted quality; the curls were loose – he felt if he pulled at one it would whang back like a spring. She moved forward a little, turning her face away so he caught a pale crescent of her neck. In that moment she was painfully vulnerable, and feeling her anxiety he moved towards her, ashamed of watching her when she was so unguarded.

He walked in a deliberate way, carefully calculated to be un-hurried without seeming over-confident or arrogant. This too was necessary for him, for without his own restraint he might rush up and grab her. She turned and saw him; she smiled a full shy smile. Her skin had a wonderful ivory sheen with the

39

pinkness of her mouth as subtle as the marking on an unbroken bud. He was suddenly afraid. She was so young, so tender, her back very straight and stiff, her face aware of its beauty but unsure of its power. The light had a strange precarious feeling to it, poised on the brink of evening, but holding the last light from the sun.

She watched his eyes as he greeted her quietly. They were a clear hazel, but it was their expression that caused her to panic. He leant towards her with a warm smile which seemed to convey his total enjoyment of her. A woman watching them felt her stomach tip in envy. He was so entirely hers, all his emotion caught in the pale oval of her face.

'Shall we walk, or would you rather have a drink?' He touched her arm briefly to usher her in the right direction. Usually Blossom had an answer to anything, but now she hesitated. He looked different away from the bright clinical lights of the Food Hall; he no longer seemed part of her world, but was a sophisticated man she knew nothing about. Even his voice seemed different, it was deeper, more Kensington than she remembered.

'Yeh, let's walk a bit,' she said, deliberately directing her own accent towards Hounslow.

They walked under the trees in Kensington Gardens and he plied her with small meaningless questions which made her feel at ease. She began to walk in the way he'd always seen her walk, with long flowing strides. You'd think she'd been brought up on the moors. She began to feel relaxed enough with him to say, 'Funny isn't it? Us being out together like this?' She gave him a sidelong look quite without coquetry.

'Is it? Why?' To him it was inevitable, simply a matter of time.

'Well, I mean, they come and go – the customers.' She swung her arms as she walked.

'Ah, I see.' He looked at the ground. 'You see me as a customer still, do you?' Laughter was beginning to surface in him and then suddenly it bubbled over in her: she was remembering how she'd been an item on his food list.

'You wrote my name down on that piece of paper, didn't you?'

'Yes, I'd waited long enough,' he said with a smile.

'Tell me,' she said quietly, 'why d'you always come in on Tuesdays and Thursdays, never other days?'

So she had noticed. 'Well, for one thing I never come in on Fridays because I hate crowds. Then there's no point in trying for a Blossom-sighting on Mondays because it's your day off.' Her thick blonde eyebrow lifted saucily. 'Once or twice I risked it on Saturdays but never saw you,' he added.

'I'm off every second Saturday.'

'Ah,' he said, 'I'm one of those people who always end up at the end of queues and are ignored by barmen in pubs, so it doesn't surprise me that I picked your days off.'

The coolness of his self-effacement was so new to her that she looked a little puzzled, but as quickly as the doubt came, it went, and she turned her face up to him and said, 'Did you come just to look for me?' Whenever she spoke, so brightly, so easily, he could see her tongue, her little teeth, the wet underlip of her most marvellous mouth.

'Of course,' he said quietly, watching the rise of her cheek which was so child-like that he wanted to bite it, in the same way as he'd often felt like gently sinking his teeth into the little plump arms of tiny girls in prams.

The scent of her skin was getting to him now, it was an indescribable smell, clean as a violet after rain; she wore no scent, no make-up.

'You're not cold, are you?' he asked protectively. There was just an echo of winter in the May evening.

'No,' she smiled at him, 'are you?'

'No,' he laughed. He longed to take her hand, but didn't; he wanted to pace everything slowly. It was more than enough to be so close to her that he could smell her, could turn his face and see her.

She was wearing a pale pink silk blouse with a navy-blue pleated skirt. He was surprised by the cut and quality of her

41

clothes, and by the impression she gave of not wearing anything beneath them. Her legs were bare, a deep creamy colour.

'Have you been at Marks long?'

'Eighteen months,' she said, 'before that I worked in a dress shop in Hounslow. I hated it,' she added simply.

'And then?'

'Then I left home. There were too many of us, what with my sister. She left her husband, you see – they only got married because there was a baby on the way. When she left him, she and the baby came back. I wanted to live and work right in town, so it was easier to leave home.'

'And M. and S. suits you, does it?'

'Yeah,' she said cautiously, 'it's good there, they treat you well. You get fed up, of course, because it's like being in school. Sometimes I think, this is a daft system or something, they ought to do such and such, but they'd never listen, or change anything. You've got to fit in, see?'

'Yes, I see,' he said, watching her bottom lip as it seemed to swell. Her proud determined glance filled him with admiration.

'You weren't always in the Food Hall though,' he said. 'I've been going there for years and I only noticed you there recently.'

'I was up on the first floor for a year, in the kids' department, until I got made up, then I went down to Foods.' There was something utterly straightforward about her.

'Made up?'

'Yeh, into a Deputy Supervisor, you get made up.'

He laughed, 'And will you stay, now that you've been made up?'

'For a year or so more, until they make me a Supervisor. There's not much point staying after that, to be a Department Manager or something. I thought I might go to America,' her cheeks dimpled as she smiled, 'I'd like that, see a bit of the world before I get too old. Most of all I'd like to have a shop, a little boutique of my own.' Her face grew wistful and her step slowed. Her ambition pleased him, particularly what it did to her face, making it glow fiercely, refining the shape.

'A dress shop, you mean?'

Her face lit up with anticipation, 'Yeh, a little shop in Knightsbridge, selling the most beautiful clothes, you know, elegant clothes that cost a fortune.' Her mouth flew open and stayed so for a while. 'That's what I want. I'd have to start as the Manageress, of course.' She turned to him eagerly, 'Once down Beauchamp Place I saw a shop with the most wonderful dress in the window, just the one, it was all silk and satin and oh, so beautiful. I wanted it, I've never wanted anything so bad as that dress, it was heavy satin, a cream, with a tiny bit of pink in it, like magnolias, it was strapless, with little gathers between the breasts and a huge floating skirt. I stood there for an hour dreaming of it, but really, mostly, I wanted to have a shop like that, and to stand inside on thick carpets with tall flowers in glass vases and make *everything* so beautiful that people couldn't resist buying the clothes.' She had talked so fast that she was out of breath, and listening to her had made him breathless.

His heart thumped painfully. He knew now that she was right, absolutely right for him.

She had checked herself, and was even a little embarrassed. He saw that her radiance had disappeared. She laughed, 'Getting carried away! But what about you? We can't talk about me all the time.' They were walking very slowly now and she was breathing in the smell of cut grass under the trees.

'What about me?' Now that he was with her he didn't even want to think about himself.

'Well, what d'you do?'

'I'm an architect.'

'Oh, very posh.' She was a little daunted – an accountant or a solicitor would have been quite enough. After a social whirl of garage mechanics, salesmen and clerks, she found herself intimidated.

'Not really,' he said lightly, 'I just couldn't do anything else.'

She laughed at this absurdity. 'You must be artistic then,' she said, and there was a note of longing in her voice.

'Only in the kitchen,' he said.

She frowned at him, dark blonde eyebrows coming closer together, 'You design kitchens, do you?'

'Well yes, sometimes, but what I meant was that I cook.'

'You cook?' Her mouth had fallen open again and he wanted to eat it.

'Yes, I love cooking. Do you?' The puzzled look on her face made her so quaint and sweet to him.

'Not really,' she laughed, 'but I love eating.'

'Well that's fine then. I love both.' A sense of relief flooded him.

'Is that why you spend so much time in the Food Hall?' she rallied like a detective.

'Apart from you, you mean? Yes. The food's very good.'

'Yeh, that's true, but it's dear though,' she said firmly.

'But worth it I think.'

'Hm.'

She wanted to know who he cooked for but was afraid of the answer. She was a little unsettled by this interest in cooking and food. Her dad cooked a bit when her mum was working late, but you couldn't ever say he liked to. Her last boyfriend – well, he'd have laughed at the suggestion even, and said, 'Sod that for a game of soldiers.' He'd said that about a lot of things. But cooking? It was a bit peculiar in a man, unless he was bent. Harold wasn't bent. You could tell them a mile off, even the half-and-half ones.

'Hm,' she said thoughtfully again.

'Can I cook for you one night?' he asked, making it sound warm and inviting, erotic almost.

She was instantly reassured. 'I'd like that,' she said happily.

'Good,' he said, 'that's settled then. Shall we go round the pond or would you like a drink now?'

'A drink,' she said, turning; her new shoes were killing her.

*

He sat her down carefully in the corner of a quiet pub. He didn't go to pubs much, only occasionally to discuss work with a client, so he didn't know the pubs in his area. He'd made a recce of all the pubs to find one specially for her. Now he saw that his choice had been sound. He turned around from the bar where he waited for drinks and looked at her; the light above her head flitted like a halo around her blonde curls and caught the soft sheen of her cheeks. She was looking around her in a wonderful eager way and he could feel her approval of the dark furniture and deep red carpets, the fluted glass lamps on the wall and the plushness of the seats.

She sipped her vodka and orange juice and smiled at him. 'It's nice here. D'you always drink here?'

'I've never been here before today. I chose it especially for you.'

She thought he was joking.

The quietness between them was as relaxing as a warm bath. He soaked in it for a moment and then said, 'Will you let me take you to dinner?'

'Well,' she hesitated, looking at a small gold watch on her wrist; she sniffed and then said, 'Well', again.

'Please do, I promise I won't keep you up late.' He quite expected her to refuse. 'Will you?' he smiled encouragingly. He wasn't assertive or insistent in any way, but the genuine feeling in everything he said made it difficult for her to refuse. She had, already, a reluctance to hurt him. She turned her face up to his again, her mouth parted so that the Cupid's bow of the lower lip was beautifully defined.

'Yes I will,' she decided impulsively and then added, 'I'm starving,' with a wide smile.

He touched her mouth very gently with the tip of his finger, 'Your mouth, I've never seen one like it, it's so marvellous.' She had the feeling, from the way he gazed at her, that he would at any moment look for a hallmark.

She shrugged with embarrassment, 'Oh, the double bows, yeh, funny, isn't it? My dad says when God was giving out lips he gave me two top ones by mistake.' She hesitated a bit, then added, 'when I was a kid I was ashamed of my mouth, people kept looking at it, you know, men and that. Funny isn't it?' Now he felt she took a certain pride in it, that it set her apart.

Her radiance came from some knowledge of her own beauty, her own worth; there was something very secure about her which he envied, and wanted.

'Well, if you're starving, hurry up with that and we'll go.' He was longing to watch her eat. He had of course already chosen the restaurant he would take her to.

It was cold outside; the stars were out and they walked down a narrow road where the plane trees were heavy with new leaves. She pushed her arm through his and said simply, 'I'll have to take your arm to keep warm – didn't put enough clothes on. It was hotter earlier.' At her touch he couldn't reply. When she turned her face the warm mass of her hair swept across his chin and he shuddered. He pushed his side tightly against her arm and adjusted his step to hers.

'I like it,' she said, 'when it stays light until late at night, like it will soon.'

'Oh, I prefer it to get dark at eight, so that night and day are properly divided.'

'Oh no,' she said firmly, 'there's too much night and dark in England.'

'You should live in a hot country,' he said, turning to look at her, 'you belong somewhere beautiful and Mediterranean.'

'Yeh?' She tipped her head sideways. 'I've never been abroad. But I know I'd like it. When I say to my mum and dad I'd like to go to Brazil or Tunisia, they say, "what d'you want to go there for?" They can't see it at all. They don't want nothing much.' Her voice was a little disconsolate.

'And you do?' he asked hopefully.

'Oh yeh. If you don't try new things you might as well be dead.'

He sensed how cramped her life must always have been,

how thin and paltry the expectations. It was heart-warming to see that she'd not become cramped by it.

'My mum says nothing good comes of restlessness and if you want more than you're entitled to, you get nothing in the end.' Her laugh was full of a confident mockery. 'I tell her I'm entitled to what I can get, and so's she – but she doesn't see that. She shakes her head at me and says, "You'll learn, girlie, you'll learn. Walk around with your head in the clouds and you'll bump into a ruddy lamp-post." Then I tell her when I come back with my pockets full of jewels and take her to the Costa Brava then she'll think different.' Her voice dropped, 'Mostly I do it, say things like that, I mean, to cheer them up – my dad specially. They might as well have cut his heart out when they took his job away – he was so proud of it. He was so different when he had a job – he used to laugh and make jokes all the time. He loved to buy us little presents. In the beginning he even made jokes about being on the dole. Not now though.'

Harold took her hand in his protectively. 'I'm sorry,' he said quietly. He thought for a moment that she was about to cry and to cover her he added, 'You will be able to do whatever you want to, Blossom, as long as you believe it.'

'Yes,' she said, raising her head and flinging it backwards so that the billowing waves of her hair seemed appropriate to her spirit, 'I want to try things, to see what's out there.' She had a quick horror as she thought of her mother in the launderette again. Then she laughed at herself, 'I've never even been on an aeroplane.' She looked ahead into the darkness and they walked on in silence.

They were outside the restaurant and the light from below a green awning made Harold hesitate a moment. He hated to be drawn away from the warm spell of the darkness and her body. She hesitated too, and he worried that she might think the restaurant too posh – though he'd chosen it most carefully: it was small, friendly, not too ostentatious. She removed her arm from his and he felt quite pained.

'Is this all right?' he asked.

'It's lovely,' she said with a stunning smile and walked forward. Then she stopped and turned quickly. He was standing so close behind her that their bodies met. They looked at one another, shocked and silent for a moment, then his arms went out and surrounded her. He could just feel the hardness of her nipples, then he pulled her closer, feeling his chest sink into the warm depths of her breasts. Her body had begun to communicate so directly with his that his mind lost its sequence. They seemed fused with a single need so fierce that with a violent movement he had crashed her body against his. It was more intimate and more telling than a kiss.

She was the first to recover. She pushed her hair back, looked at him sweetly and said breathlessly, 'Come on then, aren't we going in?' She took his hand and he followed her.

Ten

Harold walked into the calm quiet of his sitting room. He'd left a small green light on in the corner and his eyes rose instinctively to a high shelf above it where the Buddha sat serene and watchful. He sat in a leather armchair and poured himself a brandy, knowing he wouldn't be able to sleep, so there was no point in going to bed. He stretched out his long legs and rested his arms against the sides of the heavy chair. The thick red Persian rug marooned on the highly polished wooden floor filled him with a pleasure that was close to tranquillity: the subtle blues and browns woven into it formed an intricate but delicate pattern that he could watch for hours, rather as if it was a log fire, a warm centre to the room. He put on a Bowie record and, quite motionless, he listened to it.

He thought of Blossom and how she had been at the restaurant. His eyes quickened and grew less dark as he thought of how she had eaten the rosy escalope, biting into it with those milky little teeth, licking off the butter as it ran down her fingers from the haricots verts; the oil he had wiped off her chin from the golden crescents of the potatoes; the marvellous greed of her. The waiters had served and waited on her with something close to adoration because her smile and her warmth were so compelling. She'd basked in this attention, turning to look at him hesitantly once or twice to check he did not mind.

She wouldn't have the strawberries at first, because they were too dear. It made him consider the origin of the word *dear*, her use of it this way. He'd made her have the strawberries and watched as she picked one up off her plate and squeezed it gently; he knew she was judging its quality. Then she opened her lips and the red fruit disappeared into the wet dome of her mouth; he watched with intensity, as though at any moment he expected the pink flesh to cry out as she ate it. He couldn't eat for watching her; the seductive breath of the warm strawberries pierced him with longing; the juices ran into the corners of her lips and it was agonizing not to kiss her.

'Aren't you going to eat yours?' she'd said. 'You'd better or I will.'

'You are quite delicious,' he said lightly.

She laughed, leaned over pertly and kissed the corner of his mouth, 'D'you always say such nice things?'

He couldn't tell her, no never. I've never felt such feeling, such pleasure in anyone as in watching you eat. She was as basic and delicious as a simple meal – as a plump chicken cooked in butter, as fresh fish poached in its own juice, as vegetables steamed for a few minutes and eaten instantly. No, he never said such nice things because they hadn't been there to say.

Harold crossed his legs in front of him and caressed the bowl of the brandy glass, the delicate cut lines of the crystal pulled pleasantly against his skin. He frowned a little. He was trying to compare Blossom to Rachel, to what he'd experienced then; but that had been a dark and frightening passion which had pulled him to depths of sensuality that had frightened him. Rachel had tempted him with her need for excess – the extremity of her sexual needs had attracted him and then repelled him. She had demanded cruelty and her mockery of his refusals made her laugh in a horrible way that haunted him for years.

Tonight, for the first time, as he'd watched Blossom turn and wave to him before entering her door, he'd felt free, totally, of Rachel. In that one quick moment as Blossom's hand waved – Rachel had gone. Now, as he drank his brandy, he thought how it was with some women, dark women in particular, like Rachel, the idea of sex was almost sinister. It was as though they took something of you, debased it, and left you with their discontent. He suddenly shuddered to think of

Rachel with her heavy eyes and black matted hair. Then he dismissed her from his consciousness in a way he'd never been able to achieve before.

With Blossom, he thought tenderly, sex would be delicious, sex would be easy, clean – it would be ice-cream, strawberries, a white peach in honey. Her body was luscious. She was one of those rare women with an intensely exciting body smell and he knew that she would taste wonderful. He longed for her with exquisite anticipation. Deep in his groin an unfulfilled ache throbbed and pained him. He couldn't ease it as once he would have done. He suffered it, as if by this he kept her closer to him, as if his denial was an act of homage to her.

He switched off the light and went to bed, and all night long he lay awake, re-savouring her.

Eleven

Blossom was lying in the dark with her eyes closed. The door opened and Bev came creeping into the room they shared, trying very hard not to wake her. She pulled a tight T-shirt up over her head and dropped it in a chair. A black skirt with a long slit up one side followed, making a light hiss as it landed. Bev moved towards her bed and knocked over, with a resounding crash, the coffee mug she'd left there that morning. 'Shit,' she rasped. Blossom's soft giggle mingled with Bev's irritated breathing. 'I thought you were bloody asleep, I was trying to be quiet!'

'Oh yeh – that's what you call trying, is it?' Blossom said patiently.

'Well I might as well switch the light on now.'

The light between the two beds lit up a small room with an ugly painted cupboard along one wall and a pine chest of drawers beneath a window, the ledge of which was covered with pot plants and sprouting geraniums. Bev's bed had a pink candlewick bedspread over it and there was a bald teddy-bear sitting on the pillow. Blossom, curled into a bright yellow duvet, squinted as the light snapped on. Bev moved over to the mirror on the wall, her black half-slip sleek as plastic across her hips, her breasts in the big upholstered bra jutting forward like the snouts of two eager black hounds.

'Bloody hell, he's done it again!' Bev said with disgust, turning her face sideways to see her neck. 'They'll say I've been out with Drac again.' But all the same, she touched the purple love-bite beneath her ear with the softness of remembered pleasure.

'Soon it'll be liver-coloured,' Blossom said menacingly, 'then it'll turn green, then yellow, then the skin'll fall off.'

'And to think people think you're so sweet and nice,' Bev snorted. 'I suppose you've been in all night, have you?'

'Yes,' Blossom said quickly, feeling the need to straighten her pillows energetically. Her hair was tied back in a ponytail, but curls had escaped, and they overflowed around her face. 'I didn't know you were going out with the Brute tonight, you didn't say,' she said, turning over.

'Yeh, well he just turned up after work. His mum was going out and his dad was working so we had the place to ourselves. Just watched the telly and that.' She reached for some cotton wool. 'I was a bit scared one of them would come back. Last time I was there I was up in his room and his mum comes in. I'm standing looking out of the window but really Terry's into me from behind – he had to nip out so fast and course he couldn't turn round! I thought I was going to die. I'm sure she twigged. Now she looks at me like I'm a slut, but little Terry's still the golden boy of course. Though he's been putting it about since he was ten – says he owes every woman at least one turn: cocky little bastard.' She pulled at her cropped hair with a frown, 'Still, I wonder if his mum does know.'

'Course she does,' Blossom said serenely. 'Doesn't your mum know?'

'Jeez, of course not!' Bev looked horrified. 'My dad'd knock my bleeding head off.'

Blossom shrugged. 'My mum found my pills in my handbag one day, so that was it.'

'What, when you went with Martin, you mean?'

'Well who else? He's the only one I ever went with.'

'Just checking. Anyway, what did she say?'

'Well, she was a bit upset at first, but then, well, she liked Martin, hoped we'd get engaged and that. She was more upset when I broke it off with him.'

'Don't you regret it now, Bloss? I mean you've not found another fella.' Bev was pouring Baby Cream on to cotton wool and making long streaks down her cheeks as the make-up came away. Her slightly hard-looking face with the voluptuous cheeks and cherry mouth looked vulnerable stripped.

'No,' Blossom said firmly, 'I couldn't have gone on with him. He was so boring: football, his mates, the pub, rough sex.' She added the last carelessly and yet a little hesitantly. 'And talking to him was like trying to have a conversation with Tarzan.'

'They're all like that,' Bev laughed, 'poor buggers.'

'Maybe,' Blossom didn't sound convinced. She added thoughtfully, 'I know there must be more than that, there's got to be better fellas around.'

Bev sat down on her bed and flopped her nightie over her head.

'There might be,' she said, 'but where'd we find them?' She brushed her hair with short snappy strokes. 'I mean, Terry's all right, but really he's only got the one function: when he's not doing it to you he's dead boring. I couldn't live with him. Cigarette ends all over the place, clothes never picked up, and it wouldn't be safe to bend down. And he's mucky. He never washes himself after, just sticks it away, like putting a dirty sock back in a drawer.'

Blossom was laughing softly as Bev went out of the door to the bathroom, which was on the next landing. It was freezing down there, even in the summer, and a smell of drains came through the closed window. Still, they shared a kitchen with two other girls and it was better than eating and washing and sleeping all in the one room. They'd lived here for a few months and kept it spotlessly clean.

Blossom thought fondly of Bev, whom she'd known since she was twelve, when Bev's family had come to live in the flat next door. She was remembering her horror at finding Bev, aged fifteen, sitting bolt upright in her mum's bed with the man from the Prudential. Her knickers were up on top of the bed and her school blouse was all undone. She'd never walked out backwards as fast as she'd done that day. First and only time she'd ever seen old Bev embarrassed. But Bev was a good friend, the best, always there when you wanted a good cry, or a good laugh, never turned against you, never told your secrets. She loved Bev. Some of the girls at Marks thought Bev was a bit slutty – sometimes she even liked to pretend that she was: to wind them up a bit. They were so conservative and prissy, a lot of them, keeping their knees together, sitting in the backs of cars with their blouses undone to their navels, but no real sex until the solitaire was on the finger. When Bev said things like that and sneered too much, Blossom would say, 'But I bet they'll be good wives and mums and be quite happy. But what about us, Bev, will we be happy? Perhaps we should be like them?' But she couldn't, any more than Bev could. It made them both shudder to think of it: life as neatly wrapped as sliced bread, the horizons of their ambitions as clipped as the hedges of the council flats.

Now she lay on her back with her hands under her head and wondered: had no one ever told them there was more? Or was it just her, who'd never needed to be told – who just wanted, wanted, wanted. Late at night when she couldn't sleep, she would whisper: something wonderful will happen, something quite wonderful. Something that no one else can have, something just for me. One day it will happen. Oh I know it, I know it, but *when*?

Later, in the darkness, Blossom asked softly, 'You asleep, Bev?'

'Course I am.'

'What were you thinking about?'

'How it was with Terry. D'you think I'm unnatural because I like it so much? Do you, Bloss?' She was anxious and all the jauntiness had gone out of her voice.

'Course not! Don't be daft.'

'It's just that when I lie in bed I think about everything he did to me and I can feel it all over again.'

'You must love him, Bev,' Blossom said sweetly.

'Love?' Bev laughed a harsh little laugh. 'No, it's not that, it's not love. I'd know *that*.' She thought a little and said pensively, 'I think I only feel that when it's going lovely and I want it to all night. But it's like that whoever you go to bed with, at first, to do it you have to be a little in love with them at that moment.'

'But that's all?' A little splinter of light from the glass window above the door lit up Blossom's face with its soft yearning expression.

'That's all,' Bev said firmly, turning her face into her pillow and pulling her teddy-bear down into her hip. 'Course it bloody is.'

Blossom turned on to her side so that she was facing Bev, and as she did so her face fell out of its beam of light.

'You know, Bev ...' she hesitated, 'I did go out tonight, you know.' She so wanted to tell; but was so afraid that the mystery would go out of it, that the magic would fade – that Bev would stride with muddy boots all over her ballroom floor.

'Did ya? Who with?'

'A bloke who comes in at work – you know, I told you.'

'Not the one I call Jack the Ripper 'cause of his stutter? That one?'

'He doesn't have a stutter.'

'He did the day he was desperate to find you, when you'd changed departments, I felt really sorry for the bloke.'

'*You* didn't talk to him though. Who told you that?' Blossom was hot and indignant.

'Sharon did, said he was in quite a state.'

'Oh well, he doesn't anyway.'

'He doesn't what?'

'Have a stutter.'

'Must've been passion then! Go on then, tell us what happened then? Did ya?'

'I had dinner with him,' Blossom said with quiet dignity, beginning to regret this confidence, remembering that Bev's envy often made her spiky.

'Oh, *dinner*!' Bev's voice turned mocking, 'Not down the Wimpy then?'

'No, no, it was a restaurant.' Blossom hesitated, aware that now she was not going to be able to tell Bev everything. It would make her less close as a friend if there were suddenly differences between them. The idea daunted her; she'd always been able to tell Bev everything. Even about that terrible time her parents had rowed and her sweet kind dad had smashed her mum across the jaw and near bust it. The memory was still new and it hurt her, but there was no trace of pain in her voice as she said, 'Just a restaurant, nothing special.' Now the luxury of it returned to her and she suddenly found a spicy flavour in the deception.

'He's got a car then?' Bev asked, sitting up. There was a nervous casualness about her voice.

'Um, yeh.'

'What kind?' Now Bev sounded like the Inquisition.

'Well, I don't know really, a small kind of car, I don't know the kind.'

Bev was a little consoled – a Ford Cortina would have been too much. 'That's the trouble with you, Blossom, you don't notice what's important, your head's in the clouds. The least you could know was the make of the car.' Now she could be generous. 'He's nice though, is he? Sharon said he was nice looking, smallish, slim, doesn't drink beer, that's what she said.'

'How'd she know if he drank beer?'

'By the gut, dumbo.'

'Oh.'

'Well, are you going to see him again then?'

'Yeh,' Blossom said softly. After a little silence she was compelled to add, wondering at it herself, 'You know, Bev, I've never been treated like that before.'

'Like what?'

'Like, well, so nicely, like I was, well, sort of special and precious. He treated me so carefully, so nice.'

Bev was a little confused. 'Yeh? You mean he didn't try anything?' She sat up in alarm.

Blossom laughed softly again, a curious emotional tinkling laugh. 'He kissed me,' she said dreamily. She remembered it in the way Bev had described earlier, reliving even the tastes and smell, the sensations and emotions. It was such a strange kiss, starting so tenderly, like a token, a brush on her lips, and seeming as though it would end there – but then his hands had gripped her hard in the small of her back, his fists pushed into her, and the kiss was hungry, devouring, and she had to become one with it, totally submitting to it as she'd never done before. When they took their mouths back, they were both shaken and silent and her mouth buzzed and burned. He had said with a strange satisfaction, 'Your mouth is all swollen, it's so wonderful, I could eat it.'

Blossom folded her arms around herself; she felt beautiful and precious; and she felt afraid. She wanted to tell Bev what she felt, but couldn't, it was too much, too full of feelings she didn't understand. But a thought kept recurring in her head, and each time it did the echo grew more certain: I know I will be with him always. I won't ever leave him, nor him me. And with that she knew she'd been chosen, that in some unfathomable way he had chosen her, most carefully, for some purpose she did not understand.

'Bev?' she called softly, her voice like a little girl's alone and frightened in the dark. 'Bev?'

But Bev was asleep.

Twelve

Harold broke his ritual; he went to Marks and Spencer on a Saturday. He felt that if he did not see her, that day, that minute, then he would die. So he changed the order of his day. This was no small matter. His entire life was a discipline of regularity and control: the time that he woke, the hours that he worked, when he took his meals, the amount that he read – all these things did not vary. Even his idleness was ritualized. He was like a man who at every turn expects life to pull a trick on him if he's not prepared, if he hasn't worked out every contingency and done away with the dangers of spontaneity.

But here he was, plunging down the High Street, his light-brown hair swept backwards by a strong wind and his heart feeling the same turbulence. His face, without a lock of hair that fell forward on to his forehead, looked quite angular with its large nose and sensitive mouth. He looked unusually buoyant. His emotions, always a slave to him, had now made a radical shift – he'd become their slave, and this new state of affairs filled him with headiness.

This was really his day for doing things in his garden, in a leisurely way, two or three hours at the most, which he enjoyed. The lettuces needed thinning and he'd intended to plant more, and the sweet peas needed to be staked and tied up. It was also the weekend that he'd set aside to do his expenses and pay the bills. It had been so easy to think: to hell with it. And to do the only thing he really wanted to do – see Blossom, touch her again.

Even the crowd pushing in at the doors of Marks and Spencer did not deter him; he was swept along by their current. The main thrust was heading for the Food Hall and he helped its momentum by pushing and shoving himself, something he never did. His excitement and impatience to see her peaked and he felt if this was denied him he'd sink utterly.

But she was there! Beautiful in her blue pinafore with the cream polyester blouse underneath it. Her hair had large tortoise-shell combs holding it back, but the heaviness of all her curls made the hair form into furrows between the prongs of the combs. He found this lovely to look at, as satisfying as a newly ploughed field with the earth thick and chocolatey. As he stood there watching her, he knew that all those times when he'd watched her before – making no move, saying no word to her – those had been moments of the purest pleasure he would ever feel. By speaking to her that particular purity and power was broken, but a new intensity followed it. It was as if his love was being built up on layers, so, as each one was added, the one beneath gains the special glow of something fleeting, something lost, and is the more precious for it.

'Blossom?' he said, his voice catching painfully.

She looked up; she was standing next to a display of bright red apples, wicked apples, she called them, and she jumped when he called her name. He recognized in her eyes the same impatience, the same eager lurch of her body towards his. He longed to hold the emotion, to freeze it, it was so over-whelming, but it took to its heels and ran off with him.

'It's *Saturday*!' she said happily. 'You never come in here on a Saturday.'

He couldn't wait for the preliminaries; he was half-starved for the main course.

'Blossom,' he said quickly. 'Let me cook for you tonight, come to dinner, you must, you have to.'

'I can't,' she said, her cheeks flushing.

'You have to.' He didn't bother to hide his need, he didn't even stop to consider how abnormally he was behaving.

'But I'm off at two today so I can look after the baby, you know, my sister's. One of the women at the launderette's sick, so my mum and sister both have to work this afternoon.'

'Are they going to work all night?'

'Well, no, just till seven.'

'That's settled then. I'll drive you home at two and then come and collect you at eight. Is that all right?'

'You're always settling everything, you are,' she said archly, but she was pleased to be told, not asked.

'Look, I can't hang about,' she said. 'I've got to sort out these wicked reds before Sharon takes over.'

'Wicked reds?'

'The apples, like the one the witch gave to Snow White.'

'Oh, of course,' he said drolly, 'how could I be so slow?'

'Search me,' she said, 'now push off before you get me into trouble. And don't bother to take me home, it's miles. I'll get to you. Where d'you live?'

'No, I'll take you.'

'No you bleeding won't. I can come on my own legs.'

'Come on, Blossom, you'll be whacked. Here all morning and looking after a baby all afternoon. I don't want you going on the bus.'

She softened, thinking how thoughtful he was. 'No really, it's O.K., I'm used to it.'

'Blossom, I am coming to fetch you at eight, and that's final.' Never again would he be the last man in the queue.

She frowned at him, then relented. 'Look, you can come and collect me at eight as long as you stop that nonsense about taking me home too. Deal?'

'Deal.'

'Right, give us a piece of paper, quick.' She was anxious now and wrote down the address quickly after looking over her shoulder to check that Mrs O'Brien wasn't lurking about. 'It's a big block of council flats, but I'll come down, I'll be standing where you can see me. O.K.?'

'Fine, I'll go and do some shopping then. What do you eat?'

'Everything!' she said gaily, then added with a hiss, 'Get a lot,' like a greedy child being offered a treat.

'I do know how much you eat,' he said as if he'd known her for years. They walked along towards the check-outs and he leant towards her and whispered, 'I'll prepare a banquet for you.' His voice was deep and inviting. 'I'll tantalize all your senses, drown you in champagne and spread you all over with foie gras.' She was laughing at him and he knew that if he walked into a bar, he'd be served immediately. His whole life was transformed by her laughter.

'You sound as if you're going to eat *me*,' she gasped.

He bent as if to kiss her, but she stepped back smartly. 'Hey, watch it, we're not allowed to kiss the customers.'

'But are the customers allowed to kiss you?'

'No.'

'I will see you at eight, Miss Bailey, thank you for your help.'

She vanished into the displays of pineapples and melons, plump peaches and satiny nectarines, and being so much like them, she was lost to his view immediately.

Thirteen

For today I took to my human bed
Flower and bird and wind and world
And all the living and all the dead.

DANNIE ABSE

Harold stopped the car on the cobbled street and rushed round to Blossom's door, but she'd opened it and stepped out, looking down the mews at the flat-faced cottages with their tubs of wallflowers and lobelia. Honeysuckle and clematis trailed up the white or pink walls; the doors were all painted bright colours.

'You really live here, Harold?' She was delighted at the prospect.

'Yes, this one.' He led her to a green door with a number 7 on it, unlocked it and ushered her in. Immediately in front of her a very steep and narrow flight of stairs rose, turning sharply before reaching the top landing, which she couldn't see.

'Watch out for those stairs, they're lethal,' he said, directing her into the room to the left of the stairs. She walked in, feeling his hand at her back, and looked closely at the room without saying a word.

There was an old oak settle against a wall painted brick-red and, in an arched alcove, a long-legged table with a magnificent scarlet and magenta Chinese vase on it. Deep bookshelves lined two of the walls, and the grey curtains were scooped up and tied at their waists, which Blossom thought terribly grand. A glass lampshade shaped like a convolvulus gave the only light in a wonderfully intimate room filled with mellow furniture, modern paintings and delicate sculptures.

Blossom looked up at the Buddha and Harold stood quietly and watched her expression. Then she turned to him and said quietly, 'If I had a place of my own, I would want it to be like this.' Her voice was a touching mixture of awe and longing.

She ran her hand along the carved back of a Victorian chair and breathed, 'Everything is *so* beautiful.'

'The furniture belonged to my parents,' he said simply, 'my father loved antiques, he collected oak chests and settles.' His voice sounded odd, and he added hastily, 'These were just a few things they didn't want.'

'Oh, from the way you spoke, I thought maybe they were dead at first,' she said with relief. 'They're not, are they?'

'No.' His hands shook as he said, 'Here, let me take your coat.' He couldn't understand why he'd lied; it shocked him. He looked at her as she walked to sit in the throne chair that he'd bought for her as if she'd known it was hers. He felt so certain that her past was clear and bright, it seemed so obvious that she'd been taught how to love when she was tiny, by being cuddled and adored within a safe circle of faces which did not suddenly vanish. He didn't want to burden her; he wanted to protect this evening – the evening he'd anticipated so long – from the shadows of his own past.

'I'm going to make you a delicious cocktail,' he said, standing in front of her and admiring her dress. It was a vivid blue, a deep strong colour that only a complexion like hers could carry off. Her skin itself had the sheen and texture of some wonderful fabric and her body, which he could see beneath the tight bodice with its scooped neckline, had the warm, lovely smell of clean flesh. When he came back with the cocktail, she looked suspiciously into the glass and said, 'What is it?'

He handed her the tall open-throated glass and smiled, 'Well, I'll tell you what's in it – all the things you like: orange juice, vodka and a little Galliano.'

'What's that last stuff?' She still hadn't tasted it.

'A liqueur. Go on, try it.'

She swallowed it and said, 'It's strong! Good thing I've got a good head.'

He noticed how naturally she crossed her legs and dropped her arms down the heavy sides of the chair; he was thinking that the chair looked as if it had been made to set off her body to perfection.

'Are you going to look at me like that all night?' she said, flashing her eyes, 'I thought you were supposed to be cooking my dinner.'

'I am,' he smiled mysteriously, 'but will you be all right here for a minute? I have to just finish something off.'

She stood up. 'I'm coming with you.' She wasn't going to miss a man cooking in the kitchen for anything.

The kitchen wasn't large, but everything had been so carefully designed and organized that it seemed to lack nothing. The walls and surfaces were white, so were the curtains and tiles, but the tiles on the floor were a dark brick-red, and in the windowsill and above the sink long trailing green plants gave sharp splashes of cool colour to the room. She wondered if he had been married once, or whether it was just that he was an architect. Any man she knew living alone lived in a pig-pen.

'It's a lovely kitchen,' she said, running her hand along a marble slab, 'ever so clean.'

Harold, donning a large navy and white butcher's apron, began to whisk up egg whites. Blossom, not able to speak to him for the noise of the electric beater, began pressing her forefinger into the sharp crystals of some spilt sugar, which she then licked languidly. She watched as the egg whites turned silky and then grew stiff, rising higher and higher in peaks. The noise of the machine made Harold frown as he chopped, very quickly and expertly, a small bunch of tarragon.

'Can I do anything?' shrieked Blossom.

'Drink your cocktail,' he yelled back.

'O.K.' She swigged it back like lemonade, pressing her back into the cool enamel of the fridge and stretching slowly and lazily. Then she walked to the window and looked out at the

65

garden; a strong scent of lilies and wallflowers came to her as she reached out into the cool and a slight wind ruffled the wisps of hair around her forehead.

She turned to watch Harold, intense and preoccupied in his kitchen, where everything was neat with all the dirty things stacked in the sink. He seemed to reach for his knives and implements without even looking, and to be on such intimate terms with the dishes he was creating that they could only respond to so professional a touch by being perfect. Then he looked up and caught her watching him; he grinned boyishly, rubbing his hand across the brown hair that curled at his neck. His smile now turned shy, as if she'd caught him in a private devotion. The vivid blue of her dress made her eyes seem almost animal-like in their intensity. Then she flicked her hair back, and he saw an ear as small and round as a curl of pasta, and all his attention sped back to her.

He switched off the beater and relief flooded their faces.

'Sorry about that,' he said, 'I had to make you a soufflé.' His forehead crumpled apologetically, 'It'll only take a few minutes, seven, to be precise – here, have some olives to keep you going.' She took a handful. 'Now come with me,' he said, his face lighting up, 'I've something to show you.' He took her hand and led her out of the kitchen. She left it regretfully, leaving behind her the tangy smell of herbs and sizzled oil, the dark smell of garlic acquainting itself with meat.

He led her into the dining room, which was cool and mysterious, and walked towards the table to light three cream candles in tall silver candlesticks. As the flames of the candles rose higher, she could see a table upon which a banquet was laid out in her honour. She caught her breath and her cheeks grew rosy in the light as he watched her. Before her was spread an array of sparkling silver and crystal, long-stemmed white roses in clear glass vases; a bottle of champagne in a bucket of ice; crockery paper-thin and peppermint-white; silver old-fashioned and ornate. Beside each cut-glass goblet there was a decanter brimming with red wine, and in front of

Blossom's plate a cream orchid floated in a crystal bowl. Blossom rested her hand on one of the red brocade chairs and whispered in wonder, 'Did you do all this – for me?' Her eyes were filling with tears.

'For you,' he said softly, then laughed a little and confessed, 'It took hours.'

'It looks so lovely,' she came and rubbed her little velvety nose against his cheek as she kissed him, 'thank you, Harold, I feel so grand.'

Her head dropped and he kissed her tenderly on her crown, loving how her hair did not lie flat and sleek but seemed to foam about her head. He knew for certain now that he'd been right about her: the depth and sincerity of her appreciation was all the reassurance he'd been waiting for.

'Now you must sit down,' he said firmly, 'and not enter the kitchen again. You're to be waited on.' He pulled out the chair with a gallant flourish – on it was a large flat cardboard box tied with silver ribbon; she knew it was the kind of box that came from very expensive shops like Harrods. She looked at him almost with alarm.

'It's for you,' he said, 'open it.'

'Oh no I can't, really.' She stepped backwards.

'Don't be silly, come on.'

She hesitated, clenching and unclenching her hands.

'Go on, or I'll die of suspense.' He gave her a gentle nudge.

She untied the ribbons carefully, as if she intended to use them again, opened the lid, and beneath a nest of tulle and tissue, rich folds of pink satin gleamed in the candlelight. She reached into the box and lifted the cloth, her hands shaking a little. It was a wildly beautiful, wildly extravagant long dress, gathered across the bodice in delicate pleats and scooped into loose folds at the shoulders, from where the supple cloth slid down to a hem encrusted with seed pearls in the shape of a daisy chain. She gazed at it speechlessly, marvelling at it until, impulsively, she rested it against her cheek, tenderly, lovingly, as though it were a small baby. Harold watched her

with the deepest pleasure – saw how her lovely skin absorbed
the warm pinkness of the satin and the creaminess of its sheen.
She put it down, slowly, regretfully, and shook her head.

'You must take it back, Harold, it's too beautiful, I can't
have it.' The very expense of it somehow detracted from her,
caused her to question her idea of herself.

'Please put it on,' he said encouragingly. 'It's for you, no one
else could wear it. I want you to have it.'

'I *can't*,' she said with a muted anger that surprised him. He
remained silent while she looked at the floor and pushed her
feet over so that she balanced on the sides of her soles like an
awkward schoolgirl.

'Listen, why don't you just try it on? There's no harm in
that, go on, I know you'd like to. I'll just go and finish what
I'm doing.' He left the room, closing the door behind him.

The dress lay over the plush chair and beckoned her – it
seemed to be aching for her as she ached for it. She touched
the satin with her forefinger – it was as smooth as warm silver
– then picked it up to feel the weight of it and held it against
her for a moment. She put it away from her sadly, remembering some clothes of her grandmother's – nightdresses and slips
– which had the same feel and quality as this satin. A long
mirror along the narrow wall of the room caught her attention, and as she saw herself in the reflection, she changed her
mind – she began to pull off her dress quickly, telling herself
that she must be back in her own clothes by the time Harold
came back.

The deep olive glow of the heavy mirror threw back her reflection with the soft brilliance of a bottomless pool of water.
She and the mirror and the dress had become one, and when
she turned shimmers of light and iridescent colour flitted
across the glass and the satin and seemed to settle on her hair.

She felt his hands land lightly at her waist, she watched in
the mirror as the fingers spread out across her belly; she didn't
turn round but watched both their reflections intensely as his
too was sucked into the pool of the mirror. When he pulled

her back against him the reflection shattered. She tipped back her head like a cat, exposing the valley of her throat and felt his mouth sink luxuriously into the soft flesh below her collar bone. She spun round to face him, her hair grazing his eyes, her ribs taking the rough strum of his fingers. With an almost violent movement she bit him, hard, with her little sharp teeth, her milk-like little teeth, she bit him deeply across his jaw. A trickle of blood ran down his neck and with a soft moan she bent and kissed the mark, again and again, her fingers cupping the back of his neck.

The fierce excitement softened. He took and demolished her mouth like a cake warm from the oven; she felt her body slide. The dress rucked above her knees, then rose higher as her body reached the deep foliage of the Persian rug. She had nipples like oatmeal biscuits with small pink tips. Her skin seemed to be dusted with icing sugar, it smelt of marzipan. He threw off his clothes and she saw his body, shapely, flat-stomached; she reached for him and felt him sink deeply into her.

He felt he was drowning; water dragged him under so he lost his breath, but the water seemed to catch fire and he began to fight wildly, crying out with a sharp high sound. When he surfaced, the air was clear and sharp and her mouth was butting his shoulders with soft little kisses. He saw, with alarm and then tenderness, a round tear quivering on the soft down above her lip. Her tongue unfurled and caught it; he caught her tongue with his teeth and tasted the salt of her tears.

He lay still, feeling a sharp exquisite grief; he wished with all his heart that their heat would ignite and burn their bodies so that their bones would lock, never to be separated.

She shook him gently and smoothed back his hair; she looked down in dismay at the crumpled and wet dress. The smell of her was wonderful to him: a pungent oil seemed to rise from her pores as her juices ran and mingled with his; there was a scent of deep secret places in a wood. Looking at her face, it was all the same: that sweetness and purity, the innocence of her.

'Oh Harold,' she groaned, lifting up the poor dress.

'It's been christened,' he said lightly, 'and we can't take it back now.'

She knew he had never intended to, and realized with alarm that neither had she.

Fourteen

The candles had burned down, making waxy pools in the cups of the candlesticks; she unpeeled the warm shapes and rolled them between her fingers. The champagne bottle was empty and their once-crisp napkins lay crumpled on the table. He was drinking his claret and thinking what a gorgeous torpor had settled over her features.

'I've never seen anyone eat like you do,' he said approvingly. 'It's a pleasure to feed you and watch you eat – trouble is, I have to keep restraining myself from getting up and taking a bite out of you.'

She laughed, wiping her mouth with the back of her hand. He'd tied a white tea-towel around her neck and she looked like a plump cherub in a bib.

'Have I eaten so much?' She leaned back contentedly and then yawned.

'Oh – just all your soufflé, even though it was burnt, sea trout, half of a leg of lamb Duxelle, fennel florentine, boulangère potatoes and most of the syllabub.'

'Well,' she sniffed, 'I've had a busy day.' She closed her eyes and lay back with a childish smile which was wanton and innocent at the same time.

'I don't suppose you had any lunch either,' he said sternly.

She shook her head sleepily.

He watched her as she fell asleep in her chair, curled in the pink dress; her arm slipped and flopped down, making her body tip to one side. She looked utterly relaxed and he left her to sleep, remembering the dedication she'd applied to her eating and how she'd only stopped to pepper his mouth with little kisses full of the tastes of his cooking. Watching her eat had been a pure act of lust as cooking for her had been an act of love and seduction. When she woke he found to his amusement that she continued the conversation that had broken off when she fell asleep: 'You can't talk,' she said, stretching, 'you ate just as much as I did – well, almost.'

'Ah,' he said, teasing her, 'I'm what's called a gourmet, not a glutton.'

'Oh yeh? I couldn't tell the difference myself.'

She undid the tea-towel and wiped a little greasy mark off the polished table. She looked up and said shyly, 'Why d'you look at me like that?' There was a nervous thrill in the way she said it.

'Like what?'

'Like you do.' She dropped her head. 'And why,' she asked softly, 'have you done all this for me?'

'I wanted to.' He smiled at her as if she were a bowl of roses or a walled garden in sunlight. 'Because I love you.' He wasn't startled or afraid; he wasn't even shocked. He'd never lost himself to a woman before, but the feeling was so happy, so guileless, he trusted it utterly. He'd always feared sorrow and disappointment more than he'd anticipated joy – but Blossom had become so much the essence of joy that it was quite simple to love her.

'I've never had a meal like that before, tasted such lovely food, it looked so beautiful, you know, even before I ate it.' She cocked her head at him.

'Really?'

'Well, not food like that, done so – so beautifully, all those little shaped fancy bits, those slithers of cucumber that you can see through, those tomatoes like roses. You know, the way you put everything on the plate, like a painting, all arranged.' She stumbled to express it, never having known the art of food, the sensuality of it.

'You must teach me to cook like you do,' she said finally. After all, it was a bit shameful that he, a man, could cook with such skill; she wanted to be able to learn from him.

'I'd love to teach you,' he said and raised her hot hand to his mouth where he covered it in kisses.

'Don't get me going again,' she said, with a gauche little shrug.

'There's just one more thing,' he said, taking his hand back and passing her a little silver-topped dish. 'Here, these are for you.'

'Not more to eat!' She took off the cover expecting to find chocolates inside, and found instead a dish of pearls, deep cream in colour, thick as clotted cream. She lifted them out carefully, catching them in the hollow of her hand so that they clinked gently against one another. She held them up to the candlelight and saw that each pearl was differently formed, irregular, not like the pearls her mum wore with her grey cashmere sweater from Marks. The colours were soft and veiled – pink, bluish, lilac. Then she let them curl back inside the dish, and they returned to their creamy depth as if a light within their centre had been extinguished.

'They were my mother's, she had them as a child, that's why they're so small. They're Japanese.'

She picked them up again, rubbing them against her throat as a cat does with its paw.

'*Were* your mother's?' she said with a frown, 'but I thought you said – I mean, if they're hers, why do you have them?'

Lying came quickly to him, and he knew that within seconds he would almost find himself believing his deception.

'She gave them to me, I don't know why really, she was impulsive at times, it was years ago, I was about twenty. She was looking through her jewels, and she handed them to me and said, "Take these, James (she called me James you see), and keep them for the woman you fall in love with."'

Blossom flushed. 'Why does she call you James?'

'It's my first name, before the Harold. But I prefer Harold.' He'd never wanted anyone else to call him by his mother's name.

'I like Harold better too,' she said, and he loved her all the more for not encroaching any further into his past.

She pushed the bowl of pearls back to him and said, 'I think you should keep them, Harold.'

He was going to insist, but there was an uneasiness in her that made him realize that he might have gone too far. He suddenly cursed his insensitivity in not knowing she would be embarrassed if he overwhelmed her with gifts. Normally, he proceeded with such caution in all things and never risked rebuffs or false moves. He had been cautious with her too at the beginning, before daring to speak to her, watching her all those months. Now he saw how much he'd been living within his own conceptions and illusions. For him, a whole ritual of getting to know her had already taken place. He'd forgotten that she'd not been privy to this experience, that their acquaintance, upon which he'd set so much store, had gone on secretly and privately within his own heart.

The first time he'd heard her voice – how much that had revealed, the first time they'd spoken, about the lack of ripe avocados; her laugh that had shaken out a laugh from his dry throat. That wisp of petticoat; the ripeness of her sweet body as she'd walked out one evening in a turquoise dress. The kindness of her expression when she spoke to her customers; that facility in bringing out warmth and pleasure in strangers. He'd felt that he knew her, that he loved her: the whole woman – for that frill on her petticoat, the way she strode across the shop floor, her clicking heels, the hairbrush she would have somewhere full of fallen curls, the pot of cream she would use on her face at night, the lipstick that would be shaped by her marvellous mouth. He knew her intimately, but as yet she didn't know that. The pearls could wait. As he had waited.

She stood up, walked around to the back of his chair and laid her arms across the breadth of his shoulders, resting her head against his. He had a way of sitting at a table, one hand resting on his hip, that she loved. He turned to her and said, 'You must be tired – what a day you have, I don't know how you do it.'

'Yeh, Saturdays are pretty rough,' she said, walking over to a chaise longue covered in the same scarlet brocade as the chairs. She lay down on it, stretching her legs in front of her, her bare feet pointed upwards, the folds of satin slithering down to the floor. His face seemed to narrow, tightening across the jawbones, making his face slope dangerously down to the chin.

Though he remained sitting at the table, a sensual current seemed to connect them. She lay there and waited, her hand across her belly; he sat and waited, his fingers pinching the thin stem of the wine glass. The current made her hair crackle and her skin prickle. She called him. He got up quickly and walked over to her. She stretched out her arms to him and he knelt beside her.

'Kiss me,' she said fiercely, coiling her arms about him, 'kiss me.'

Her beautiful mouth, for all its voluptuousness, had something secret and sad about it; it made him think of sleep. Her eyes, half-closed, seemed to be lost to him and terror filled him, a premonition of grief.

'Blossom,' he called, with a voice shaken with fear, 'don't leave me.'

She neither understood his grief, nor its source, but her arms took him to her tightly and held him with a warmth that banished ghosts, with kisses that rocked him back to safety.

Fifteen

While she lay sleeping on the chaise longue, he cleared the table quietly and stacked the dirty dishes in the sink. Then he went back and knelt beside her, watching the warm laziness of her body as she slept, the heaviness that had settled on her once quick features. He could see her eyes flickering beneath her eyelids and once or twice she smiled in her sleep, tilting her face upwards.

The satin had risen, showing the sumptuous flesh of her knees. He lifted the heavy cloth and looked at her thighs, they lay tenderly side by side, almost prim. He lifted the cloth a little higher and brushed his hand very gently against the mound of hair, seeing its dark gold colour, seeing how it grew, dividing itself into two waves at the tip of the triangle.

She woke suddenly, pulling her dress down with an awkward gesture, frightened by such intimacy. She began to grow flustered like a very young girl. He cuddled her and said, 'Come on, it's time I put you to bed.'

She unwound in his arms and was led off, drooping, to bed. He'd turned the covers down for her and left a pitcher of water in case the champagne and claret made her thirsty in the night. She allowed herself to be undressed and then curled into the deep bed, into the warm hardness of his body, and all night long he lay deep inside her, safer than a child in the womb.

Sixteen

Blossom woke the next morning to see him lying on his side watching her tenderly. The sun twirled through the windows, playing on her hair and making it seem to ripple. She reached out and stroked his cheek. Then yawned and stretched deliciously, throwing back her arms with her hands clenched into fists.

'Oh I could stay in bed with you all day,' she sighed, turning and wrapping an arm across his chest.

'There's no need to get up,' he said, 'everything you need is beside you.' She turned round to see a small table with a white tablecloth on it, freshly squeezed orange juice, grapes, croissants, honey, curls of butter in a china shell and two fat aspirin next to a glass of water. She could smell real coffee toasting in the kitchen. A cool breeze wafted through the opposite window.

She gave a little cry of delight and covered her face with her hands. 'I can't believe it,' she said. 'I thought this morning that last night was something I dreamt, and then there you were beside me!' She looked across the room and there, on the chair, the pink dress was stretched out as though exhausted.

'I should have made *you* breakfast,' she said reproachfully, 'I have to do something for you.'

'What on earth for?' he said lazily. 'Now, if you'll just sit up I'll arrange the pillows behind you. Then I'll get the coffee.'

'No, you will not,' she said vehemently, 'I will.'

'O.K.' He surrendered easily, lay back and watched her as she leapt out of bed. The sun flung itself at her naked body; her skin seemed to lick it up like litmus paper. Then she disappeared into the corridor.

She was pouring honey into the soft inside of a warm

croissant; she was embarrassed to say what she wanted to say, so decided to duck behind a façade of nonchalance. 'Harold,' she said quietly, but matter-of-factly, 'I've never been licked before.'

'Yes I know,' he said softly, 'you were frightened at first.'

'Hm,' she said, now wishing to change the subject. She sucked the honey spoon in a way that made her lips disappear.

She thought how strangely but wonderfully he made love to her. How unlike the rushed thrustings of her past, against walls, in the backs of cars. Her pleasure then had been as much the fear of discovery coupled with the hot pain of those rammings which paid no heed to her own rhythms. Sex with Martin had been fast and forlorn; they'd never spent a complete night together; he had never learned how to treat her physically or emotionally.

'You taste delicious,' Harold said, untangling a strand of hair which had forced its way into the corner of her mouth. He leant forward and bit his favourite part of her: the little scallop of flesh below her collarbone. As he kissed her throat, her smile was a mixture of pleasure and apprehension, and sharp quivering sensations travelled down her body to her thighs. He was pleased that no one had tasted her before, though surprised, because she was so edible; nor did it bother him that she was not a virgin after she'd shyly confessed that she'd never had an orgasm before.

Sometimes, when she jerked, pulling him into her, he wondered whether she wanted him to hurt her. This for a moment terrified him, and the dark image of Rachel returned with her hoarse voice groaning uglily, 'Fuck me, fuck me.' But with Blossom that hard passion united them; it did not exclude or use him. He couldn't hurt Blossom, the thought of it was repellent to him. That time, on the chaise, when she lay there, replete and voluptuous, there had been an abandoned quality in her that had excited him – as that passionate bite had excited him. He felt it was new to her, a discovery of her own sexuality that was only possible because of the way he protected her, smothered her with care and gentleness.

'Oh Harold, you're so lovely,' she now said, 'you're the nicest one in the world and I love you. I love you, I love you.'

She came out of the bath wrapped in a warm pink towel; her cheeks were rosy beneath the aureole of wisped hair. He had showered quickly as she bathed and was now dressed.

'Shall we go for a walk in the country, Blossom, would you like to?'

'Oh yes,' she curled into her towel with pleasure, 'but I must ring Bev first or she might ring home looking for me and my mum thinks I'm with her.'

'Yes, of course, I'll bring the phone over for you.' He walked over to the rosewood table between the long curtains and picked up the phone.

'It's like a luxury hotel here,' she said, wriggling her toes in the thick woollen pile of the beige carpet and looking up at the dark blue ceiling. As she took the phone from him, she said chattily, 'Bev's a bit of a worrier, you see, if I didn't go to work or something, when I was living at home I mean, she'd be on the phone in a flash.'

'Do you think she might have rung your home already?'

She laughed and tucked the end of her towel under her arm. 'Not a chance, not on a Sunday, Bev sleeps till twelve on Sundays, so we're all right.'

He liked the way she said 'we' and included him in this way.

'Yes, we'll drive to the country in about an hour, the sun's shining,' he said, full of the eagerness of a man planning how to spend the rest of his life with one woman.

'And a picnic,' she said, putting her hand over the receiver, 'with cold lamb sandwiches and chutney – I think I left a little bit over.'

'And strawberries and cold wine and cheese.'

'Yes, and then we'll come back and watch the Sunday matinee,' she said happily. And his heart quite overflowed: she

79

was a beauty, a perfect peach of a girl. He came and sat beside her and dried her pretty back, noticing the little crater on her arm where an inoculation needle had blighted the skin.

Bev still hadn't answered the phone, which was out on the landing, so Blossom had time to say, 'Harold, I will have to go back this evening, you know.' She sounded apologetic. 'It's the Brute – that's Bev's fella, he goes out with his mates on a Sunday evening and she'll be lonely if I'm not there.'

'Of course,' he said, 'whatever you like.' The first return of loneliness hit him.

Bev had answered and now Blossom was talking to her. He noticed the edge of strain, or reserve in her voice now, as if she was being pulled in another and opposite direction, away from him. He saw how her hand nervously fretted with the sheet and then went up to stroke the brass of the bedstead, and how she sifted out her words when normally she chattered on so gaily and fast. He noticed too that her voice had picked up a slight roughness from the voice on the other end of the line.

He walked slowly to the kitchen, his brow pulled down with anxiety as he wondered how he could help her with the problems he must be creating in her simple life. It was this very simplicity that he'd wanted from her, with its echoes of a gentle time in his childhood – being cared for by a blonde country girl who'd held and cuddled him through his nightmares. Now, by becoming part of Blossom's simple life, he could see how he might destroy it.

But when she came in, she said laughingly, 'Bev's jealous, I bet you! She's trying to be cross with me because I'm having such a good time – not that I told her everything, that'd drive her round the twist.' She nudged against him like a puppy and began filching the strawberries he was carefully putting into a punnet. He was flooded by relief.

'Back!' he growled, 'those are for the picnic.' She kissed his neck and ruffled his hair. His doubts vanished, his fear went up in the whoosh of sunlight that had entered the kitchen with her presence.

Seventeen

But that night, after she'd gone, it was different. He tried to summon her back: he lay on the bed and smelt her, he could see her face as it had lain on the pillow framed by her hair. The image of her face lingered, and it seemed to him this time that he saw her face white and haunted as if behind a pane of glass. His body shuddered with a sudden fear for her, as if pushing too hard on that pane could shatter her pale reflection.

The night trailed by, hour after deadly hour. He walked, he sat and drank brandy, he listened to some Brahms, but nothing eased him. He ran upstairs to the cupboard and pressed his face into the pink dress hanging there; he breathed her in, he had her. For a little while he felt safe again.

But when he got into bed and lay there, he knew he wouldn't be able to sleep. He knew it would be another of those insomniac nights when he had no control over the visitations that would come to him in that murky, drowsing state. His need for her grew wild and sick; he had no hope of tomorrow, he didn't trust life, or his ability to influence its unpredictabilities.

Her warm stillness of the night before – how could he have so soon got used to the utterly feminine contours of that body, so that now he was utterly dependent upon it? He, who slept alone so much, and did not adjust well to the sleeping undulations of women, was now quite lost without her. He got up and began to pace the room.

He was afraid: love had the power to destroy. He knew it. He'd known it as a boy rushing out of the school door to his mother's familiar shape and burying himself in her thighs with relief at the end of the day. And later, in the car, he remembered saying, 'I love you *so* much. If you were dead and I wasn't I'd cry for ever. I'd have to die too. You won't die, will you, you won't?'

Her wistful face, with the oddly expressionless eyes and the lock of fair hair that always lay across one eye, had turned to him; she'd held his hand and said, 'You say such odd things for such a little boy. What a strange little boy you are.' And she'd laughed softly.

Love was not new to him: he and his mother had existed as one person, all in all to one another like one flesh. And then, without warning, she was torn from him. She just disappeared. She never took him to one side and said, 'James, I am going away for a while, but I'll be back, I promise I'll come back.' She just went. And as soon as she'd gone, everyone ceased to speak about her, it was as if she didn't exist. The cook took over, and if he asked her about his mother, she shushed him and gave him a biscuit. Once, he'd plucked up the courage to ask his father, who'd looked up from his huge desk and said, 'She'll be back. Don't worry about it. Go and play.' But he didn't trust his father; he blamed his father for her absence.

Later, he began to see that these absences affected his father too. He became angry and forgot his appointments. He left his patients waiting in the surgery, and when reminded about them, he went out slamming the door, and came back with sand from the beach all over his shoes and his grey hair as stringy and forlorn as his face. But no one mentioned this either.

When his mother did come back, she slept a great deal. She looked thin and tiny and sometimes in the night she came and took Harold from his bed and carried him to hers. She held him painfully against her all night, so tight that he felt they had become one person again. In the morning there were marks where her fingers had pressed into him. But he didn't mind. He would have borne anything to keep her, to keep her always with him. But as soon as he'd got used to having her with him, as soon as he began to feel it his right, she would go again. And again, and again.

Harold slept for a little and woke to the sound of his own cry – a desolate eerie sound: a child trapped in a man's body. He remembered, long ago, waking in the night, a small pale boy with huge eyes. Hearing the blue china clock with blue birds on it going tick, tock, tick, tock. The night's heartbeat. He knew something terrible was happening in the silence.

'Mummy? MUMMY? Oh Mummy, I want my Mummy.' His scream colliding with the white walls, with the hard shiny panes of the moonlit windows.

'Get up! Get up!' Who whispered that? Did she call him? Did she walk to him? The night was dark and sticky, it would wrap around and suffocate him. Not a sound.

'Mummy!' She walked to him, so thin that through her body he could see the pale curtains blowing. No breath, no breath departing. She walked to him, their bodies became one in the white glow.

His father carried him back to bed; he was shivering as if with fever. His father took care of him. But his face was awful, like the devil's – it was turned against itself. When he spoke his voice was not his own, but a rasping breathless sound.

He had slept and woken again, risen from his bed and walked to his mother's room. The long bureau was lit by a single switch of moonlight. Beside her bed, on a chair, was a silver knife. And on a plate, a peach. He lifted it and rubbed it against his cheek, he kissed it. The bed was empty, smoothed. He held the peach and began to cry for his mother, violent sobs shaking his body as though someone shook him. He climbed into the bed and lay there, sobbing, stuffing the sheet into his mouth because it smelt of her. Much later, when it was dawn, he sat up, half-awake, half-asleep, and with the knife he cut a single slice of the peach. He placed it in his mouth and chewed it, gently, slowly, until it had all gone.

He was never told what had happened to his mother and he never saw her again. It was simply not discussed. It was marked only by the total alteration of his father. His father became a Catholic. His life centred around daily Mass and his prayers, his withdrawal, his silent desperate addiction to the Church. And then, one day, he decided that Harold too must become a Catholic. And from a childhood devoid of religion, Harold was pulled, at the age of seven, into the rigours and rituals of a frantic and terrifying Catholicism.

Eighteen

Once a Catholic, always a Catholic. Oh my God, what have I done? What have I *done*? I'm sweating, I'm so terrified I can barely breathe. And the telephone has begun to ring and ring. I can't answer it. I can't even move.

I must try to think straight, to understand. But I *do* understand: I was mad with grief, I became that boy of six again, torn of all hope. So why this pandemonium of doubt? I can't bear to question myself any more, it would be fatal. I couldn't survive it.

Oh Blossom, if only you were here to reassure me; to hold me against you. Sometimes I feel you have really left me; then my despair is frightful. I go and find you in your clothes. As once, when a child, I clattered around in my mother's slippers, stole her hankies, wrote with her brown pencils and put the powder puff that had touched her cheek down my shirt and felt it there all day. I can be intellectual: I can still remember things without letting their emotion destroy me. *Now* I can do that. It won't last.

I keep remembering how you said you would never leave me. How did you so uncannily pick the very words that I could never believe in? They are His words: *Lo, I am with you always. Even to the edge of doom.* When those words were first said to me, I hated them with all my heart. It wasn't Jesus I wanted at seven, it was my mother. When they placed that little wafer on my tongue, it was not Jesus, it was her I took inside me. *Take, eat, this is my body, this is my blood. Do this in remembrance of Me.* In remembrance of you, Blossom, in remembrance of you. Oh Blossom, this is too wounding, I cannot bear it. Let me creep back to the covers of the past, because though I hate it, I hate the present even more violently. Because I have lost you, oh my Blossom.

But I must tell you these things, Blossom, so that you can understand what I've done, and perhaps I will too. Every Sunday at Mass, my mother and I became one again; she was returned to me and I began to believe in the words, *Lo, I am with you always*. She came back to me with that wafer, she lived inside me and kept me safe from the world, from the grief-stricken man who had gone white, who had grown old, who drove home in the old Rover from Mass speechless with some furious hope that had snatched him back from death. For death wasn't far from him – I knew that when his days were spent in a darkened room, my mother's room, and no one came to the surgery and when in the night I heard him beat his head against the wall and shriek softly for his God.

Then my mother's sister came, and I heard her say angrily, 'It's not in the family, how dare you! There's nothing wrong with any of us, no one's done anything like that.' Then she added malevolently, 'It wasn't *her* fault, now was it? Was it?' My father almost bodily threw her out and she never came again. She took my mother's things with her, all except the ones I had secreted away: the pencils, the pearls, the hankies and powder puff. It broke my heart to find all her dresses gone, no longer the comforting lengths of satin and wool to cry into.

My father barely spoke to me after that: perhaps he couldn't bear to see her imprint on my face. But by finding God and the Catholic Church he was pulled back to life with a rapturous frenzy close to madness. It was a madness born of desperation. He called it a conversion. Perhaps it was: a conversion to life again after death had beckoned him so fiercely.

But I hated God. I thought of Him as a kidnapper, and the sweets that the holy father, his accomplice, offered me went into my pocket, and later, all furred, I would throw them vehemently away. Heaven and hell were laughable concepts to me. I brewed my own private religion from the stock of theirs – but my God was a woman. I found her easily in the incense and soft chanting, in the vases of carnations and roses and the gleaming silver, and if ever I needed an intercessor then it was Mary, whose statue in the chapel looked strangely like my mother. I was happy then for a little space: I loved the rituals and the beauty of the words, I loved the way the music and the slowness of time made me dream I was in heaven. But I could not forgive God.

And now I can't forgive myself. No one can live with that – not even I, who developed so young a self-control that was almost inhuman.

Have I become inhuman again?

Nineteen

Blossom, I don't care if they don't understand, as long as you
do. I keep remembering that conversation we had. We had a
picnic in the woods; we were lying on the grass, your head was
in my lap – it fitted perfectly, we always fitted perfectly. You
looked up at me, then closed your eyes and whispered, 'Just
then, when your hands tightened around my throat and you
kissed me so hard I couldn't breathe, I thought: perhaps he will
kill me? And then I thought, I wish he would, if only he would
kill me like that. Because nothing more beautiful could happen
to me.' I thought of it as a homage, an act of total communion.
It became a ritual of ours – to peak higher and higher – for
me to almost suffocate you with my mouth and then you
would surface with a sharp clean cry like a dolphin. It was a
dangerous and beautiful ritual, as frightening as the power we
had come to have over one another.

We began to talk of strange things that day. I told you about
Rachel and how she'd made me tie her up so tight that the cord
cut into her and how it sickened me and I refused, so that she
attacked me. I knew then, in telling you about it, that that was
what Rachel had really wanted – to attack me. You couldn't
believe I could treat anyone badly, particularly a woman.

Thinking all this, I am close to you again. I love you so,
Blossom. I loved the way you spoke and the way you rolled
over on the sides of your feet and ran your finger under your
nose in that sweet vulgar way. And your mind, I loved that too,
sometimes it was as spicy and fresh as an orange. You were
often utterly ordinary – I'd had enough of complicated women
– but sometimes, when we'd talked a long time, a perverse
thread, an unconventionality surfaced in you. You became
quirky, you wanted new thoughts, new experiences – you

wanted more, more, more. And I wanted to help you find it.

Then we had that strange conversation. It all started quite simply. You were laughing at the way I snapped the chicken bones with my teeth and made plum stones explode in the same way. You said I'd make a good cannibal. I said I wouldn't leave any of you untasted. Then you grew serious and began to think of that plane crash. You said you would eat someone if you felt you were dying. Oh, what did you know of dying – of death – on that bright sunny day? But you were serious, the idea did not revolt or appal you.

I said: 'If I were dead and you were dying, would you eat me?'

'Yes, I would, I'd eat you lovingly, I'd take you into my mouth as you've taught me – it would turn me into a gourmet.' You laughed a blithe leaping laugh, then whispered, 'We would be the same then.'

That's what you said, Blossom, and I hold to your words. Because there are many ways of dying; you taught me one, I taught you another. And I was dying, Blossom. Dying for you. So close to it I tasted it. Forgive me, please forgive me.

Twenty

Blossom, if what I did was mad, it was the action of a man driven mad by sorrow. This is a sane space, so I know it. But I feel myself falling and the sane space shrinking. Blossom, you are too far to help me now so I must creep back to a dark place where I can hide my sorrow. I must hide it deep till I am strong enough to bear it.

Oh my Blossom, come back to me, come back to me now, for one moment.

Twenty-one

When Harold woke, it was as if the long dark night hadn't happened. He felt peaceful, almost happy. This surprised him; normally after he hadn't slept he woke feeling depressed and edgy. But this morning he couldn't even be bothered to work: he wanted celebrations, holidays, banquets again. He wanted Blossom.

He sat at his desk and relished the idea of devoting a morning to thinking about her. He smiled to think how determined and definite she could be. She'd told him, almost like drawing up terms of an agreement: 'I'll only stay at the weekends, because during the week I like to wake up in my own bed. I've never been one to be always with one other person all the time, like Bev – she sees the Brute nearly every night. That'd drive me crazy. I like some nights to myself. I like it when Bev's out and I can be by myself.'

He didn't know whether to be relieved that she had his own familiarity with solitude, or whether to feel threatened by it.

'So what do you do when you're on your own?' he asked.

'Oh, I sit and think, and plan my shop. I might be going to learn French at a night-school, and Bev and me thought we might go to a place in Hammersmith that teaches modern ballet. I'd *love* to be able to do that! Sometimes, I just lie on my bed and dream, sometimes I like to go to bed really early and read. Other times I walk in the park, or walk down the expensive streets looking for a dress shop just for me. I go and choose one, you see, I like the look of a certain one and I bag it and say, that's mine. Then I have something definite in my mind to think around.'

She'd made it clear to Harold that her life was her own, that there was a place for him in it, but that it mustn't wipe out her space. He did understand it, but understanding didn't stop his fear of her separate existence.

As he sharpened his pencils and replaced them carefully in a long box, he decided that really they were quite alike: independent, self-sufficient. He was probably more solitary, but he wasn't exactly unsociable. Sometimes he felt he ought to make more of an effort, get out and see people, but he did it rather in the nature of taking a necessary dose of humanity for his own good. The benefits were slight. There was something about being in a crowd of people that made him feel inadequate, but slightly superior at the same time. It always rather surprised him when people singled him out, wanting to see him, taking his telephone number, which for some curious reason often escaped him at these moments. Women found him gentle and attractive; the shrewder ones detected a quiet mockery in his smile. He had no close men friends. Apart from Julian, who was only close because of the length of time between them.

It was in fact through Julian that he was to go and see a prospective client that morning. A Greek woman who wanted her flat in Kensington re-designed. Julian said he knew her too well to take her on himself: she was a pain, but Harold would be able to handle her. Besides, Julian sighed, he wasn't going to knock himself out working for someone else; he had enough to keep him ticking over quietly.

Harold knocked at the door of the Greek woman's flat at precisely eleven o'clock. A maid in a short black skirt, with chicken-like legs, also draped in black, led him in without smiling. He summed up the position the minute he saw his new client. She wore a black silk robe and her hair was scraped back, black also and very thick. She was talking on the phone, waving her arms frantically, babbling half in English, half in Greek, laughing, then shouting, until finally she was reduced to a furious outburst of bilingual expletives and insults. He had been waved downstairs and the large room he waited in was like an amphitheatre which played out a distant but noisy Greek tragedy.

Harold did not like being kept waiting; he was never late himself. Just when he was wondering how to convey his displeasure at the continuing delay, in she walked, a curious agitated flinging of her arms accompanying her.

'Mr Moreton, I have kept you waiting.' The accent was thick as Greek coffee at the bottom of the cup and just as grainy. 'I had some problems,' she waved her hand in a wretched way. Sensing he might be pulled into these, he began briskly, 'Julian said you wanted some changes done to your kitchen, and to your bathroom too, as I remember.'

She brightened. 'Shall I tell you how I chose you?' she asked in a low seductive way. 'We were at a party, John, my fiancé, and myself. A man looked into a room, a conservatory, with glass and plants and those things, and then he said, "This must be a Moreton." He recognized your touch, you see, and I thought: Ah, he is talking of an architect like an artist, this is the man I want for my little plans.'

She waited for the response, but there was none, so she continued, 'Not that I am wanting things built so much as in that house – you built a whole new wing there and we were celebrating that night with the party. Yes?'

'Yes.'

'It's magnificent, I love it!' Arms and silk robe flew into the air and fluttered there. Compliments alarmed him, also he couldn't bear her insincerity, so with a quick smile, he tried to head her in the right direction.

'But you, you wanted your kitchen enlarged and modernized – do you think I could see it?'

'But of course. But first the bathroom, while the servant makes the coffee. I say servant – you don't mind – it was living in Cairo – I can't change now.' The thick mushroom-coloured carpets led to the bathroom and stopped there. 'I need more space in here, I'm sick of this bathroom, I need a bidet and a bigger bath, you understand? It must change or I want a new house. I want to make it nice for my new husband when he comes; we are to be married quite soon.'

93

'It's a very nice large flat,' he said, feeling a little exchange was necessary and unavoidable. As she gabbled on he tried to remember what Julian had said. Something about her marrying a young banker, and how she liked to seal her emotional arrangements with cash investments. He began to listen again because it was being made clear to him that the fiancé was to pay, and that the more it cost the greater the value she would consider he'd placed on her.

When they'd pored over pictures she'd torn from *Vogue* and *House & Garden*, with her scribbles all over them, he suggested they look at the kitchen.

'Ah, the kitchen' she said with disdain, 'that was here when I came. Terrible taste,' she added, hoping to excuse her past.

'You lead the way,' he said.

She threw open the door, startling the servant, and pleaded dramatically, 'So tell me, Mr Moreton, can you do anything with this little cage of a kitchen?' He looked around a room that could have floated a small cocktail party and decided he was going to wind up this visit as fast as he could drink the coffee.

An hour and a half later he left the house, his head reeling, her accent repeating as unpleasantly as a radish. He was utterly exhausted. He couldn't imagine why he'd agreed to come back and do the specifications and plans. Of course she was an impossible woman; the job would drive him to distraction; she'd never be satisfied; she'd feel free to ring him up on Sunday mornings and complain, and he was pretty certain that old friend Julian hadn't bothered to check out whether the young banker actually had any money. And she was exactly the kind of client who'd drive his builder, Max, round the bend. He'd have to get her right out of the place when the work was being done. Still, he'd told her he couldn't take it on until next month. And he had worked for women like her before. They were just about manageable if you remained aloof and professional and told them what they wanted. Then she could see it as an investment even if she ended up not liking it. And some money up front, that was definite.

He drove home to find it was well after one, which annoyed him as he always had lunch promptly at one. Also, he had to be with Max in Holland Park by two-thirty. Fortunately, he'd stopped earlier that morning at the delicatessen. He laid out a ripe avocado, some Brie, olives, tomatoes and French bread on the scrubbed table in the kitchen. The woman had come and done the cleaning and there was nothing to show that Blossom had stood there by the table eating strawberries, chatting to him. His house was unchanged by her existence, his working life was too – it was as if she had utterly forsaken him.

As he sat at the dining table he found himself remembering things he'd convinced himself he'd forgotten. Himself as a child going into the big back garden, closing his eyes and holding out his arms and calling for his mother. He was certain she'd come back, that she'd creep up behind him as she used to do, and say, 'Boo, I got you!' When she didn't come and his voice began to falter and tears stung his eyes, he ran desperately into the kitchen and began to shove food down his throat – anything, everything. He ate and ate and ate, but it was as if a hole grew inside him. He could see himself as he'd been: attacking the food ferociously with knives that he was too young to handle, chopping it and devouring it like an animal. These memories were so agonizing that he couldn't eat and his stomach seemed to twist and churn as it must have done then.

His feeling of disorientation only left him when softer memories blurred out the painful ones; when he could think of the time when the young woman came to look after him. She had pale hair and a sweet face. She didn't speak like Harold and his father spoke and he smiled to think how his father had said she held her knife like a pencil, as if this was as serious a crime as calling the lavatory the toilet.

The past lost its grip – but a sadness remained as he remembered how she and he made little cakes in the kitchen and she let him ice them with pink and white icing sugar. Little by little she had filled the void in him. He could sleep at night if she sat and held his hand; his nightmares were less frequent. She put the blue clock with the china birds away because it frightened him. He even began to eat like a normal boy; his eating began to comfort him whereas his frenzied feasting had emaciated him; he'd choked on it and sicked it up. Finally, he even grew a little fat.

He remained sitting at the table as the clock announced that he would be late for his appointment with Max. He barely noticed; he was thinking of Blossom, missing her desperately, feeling as if a door had closed against him. The extremity of his feelings frightened him. He struggled with all his intelligence against his unruly emotions, but was left feeling only a bewildering and painful connection between love and loss which no amount of rationalizing could shake off.

It was only when he realized that there wasn't any point in going to the meeting with Max, because it was far too late, that he saw, and was shocked to see – that Blossom's existence *was* in fact changing his entire life. He'd never missed a meeting before; he'd never felt so uninterested in a job as he had been that morning at the Greek woman's flat. All that now mattered was Blossom – when he could see her, when he could touch her again.

When the shock of this wore off, he grew excited by it. Because nothing would ever be the same again. He decided that it must be the most glorious and liberating thing that could happen to a man: to find his entire life changed by the existence of a woman.

He rang Max to tell him he wasn't coming, then went into the garden and fell asleep in the sun.

Twenty-two

Blossom unclipped the key from the ring at her waist and opened her locker. Slightly to her left Bev threw off her shoes with a 'Jeez, I wish someone would untie my feet and hang them up. What a day!'

Blossom pulled the navy-blue pinafore up over her head and sent her curls dancing. Her blouse was folded and put tidily in the locker with the pinafore. She shook out, then flopped over her head, a turquoise dress made of stiff cotton; it had long loose sleeves tucked at the wrists into tight cuffs, and a broad belt. Instantly she became at odds with her surroundings; she was something exotic among the rows and rows of grey lockers with hanging areas, the lengths of mirrors, the trampled carpets and the hurly-burly of young girls' bodies – fat and thin, sweet or smelly – all changing to go home. She was like a sapphire fallen among cabbages.

Blossom glanced about her and was surprised, once again, that some bodies, young bodies, should look so marked so quickly – stretch lines, loose fat, blotchy skin. She felt a new awareness and pride in her own body which she'd barely considered before. Then, just as quickly, she forgot it. She walked over to Bev, who, because she was involved in a conversation with Tracy, was only just beginning to unfasten her buttons.

'Yes, well I don't feel sorry for her,' Bev said sternly, turning to Blossom, 'talking about Annie getting caught after taking a thousand quid from the tills. I mean, she'd been up to it for months and her mum and sister was in on it too.'

'How'd they do it?' Blossom always got the gossip from Bev.

'Used to hand over "change" in ten- and twenty-pound notes. Her mum or sister came in, bought something small when Annie was on the till, she rings it up and then hands over lots of large notes.'

'It's so stupid to do it,' Tracy said, strapping on her sandals, 'they always get 'em in the end.'

'Well that's the end of her life,' Blossom said gloomily.

'Yeh, the cops came and took her off, now she's got a record; she'll have to pay the money back, too.'

The three girls shivered, feeling the chilly breath of their own temptations.

'Funny,' Tracy said, 'I never think of it as money.' She peered into a little mirror and put on some bright red lip-gloss with her fingertip. 'It's just sort of paper or something now.'

Bev agreed, the pinafore finally coming off, exposing her hard-set flesh in the beige nylon slip.

'I do feel sorry for one thing though,' Bev said moodily. 'She's got a kid. Little boy. What with her mum and sister and Annie in trouble, who's gonna look after the poor little bleeder?'

'She should have thought of that,' Blossom said. 'You've got no business doing things like that with a kid. Her mum must be a bad lot too. What about her boyfriend?'

'Out of work. They don't know if he was in on it or not because he's scarpered.'

'He's a sweet little boy. I remember once she brought him in,' Blossom said sadly, 'you know, lovely shiny black hair, all thick like, just like Annie's.'

'Yes, poor thing, poor Annie, being such a bloody fool.'

'What she do with all the money?' Blossom said, walking back to make sure she'd locked her locker properly.

'Bought all this furniture and stuff. Have to give it back, though.'

'You ready then, Trace, Bloss? Let's get out of this bloody place and get a smell of fresh air.'

They had a drink with Bev, who had an hour to kill before the Brute came to collect her. They sat in a corner and drank vodka and orange, apart from Tracy, who was dieting again.

She was a plain, stocky girl, but her eyes were bright and pretty. Her hair was cut short one side and long the other – like you got it caught in a hair-dryer, Bev said, when she was having a go. Tracy was so daft you could take the piss out of her for hours and she'd never know it, but she was so sweet-natured also that both Bev and Blossom liked to have her around.

'What's the matter with you, Bloss?' Tracy said, watching Blossom twirl her glass around in a puddle of spilt beer that they'd inherited with the table.

'Oh don't mind her,' Bev snorted, 'she's in love.'

'Yeh?' The plain face lit up as though someone had lit a candle behind it. 'Who with?'

'Time will reveal all,' Bev said mysteriously, lighting a fag. (What she and Blossom knew, she and Blossom knew.)

Blossom shook herself slightly. Then she leaned forward, winked, put on her music-hall face to make them laugh, and whispered, 'O.K. I'll tell you then, shall I?'

Tracy leaned on the table with her elbow and said, 'What? Go on, tell us.'

'Well, it was like this. I met a really dishy fella the other night. He's got a really big flashy car, a Jaguar, sort of silver colour. Bev can give you the technical details.' She shared a private look with Bev, who threw back her head and inhaled deeply.

'Yeh, well go on, what happened?'

'Look, you've got your sleeve in the slopped beer,' Bev pointed out.

Tracy brushed it off impatiently and repeated, 'Well, go on then, hurry up about it.'

'O.K.' Blossom thought hard. 'Well, last weekend, see, he drove me down to Brighton in his Jag; we stayed in this really grand hotel, then we went over the sea to Calais and ate oysters and drank champagne out of his hat and he gave me a red rose for every curl on my head and ...'

'Give over Bloss, you just don't want to tell me, do you?' Tracy said quietly, in a hurt voice.

Blossom repented immediately, 'Oh, I'm sorry Trace. Look, it's just a nice fella I met, that's all.'

'He's old though,' Bev chimed in.

'He's thirty-one,' Blossom said, quick as a flash.

'One foot in the grave; they're in their prime at seventeen,' Bev said mournfully, looking round the pub. 'Can't get it up more than once an hour after that, ready for the scrap-heap.'

'Bev, shush,' Tracy said with a giggle, 'someone'll hear you – look, that bloke over there with the greasy hair and flared trousers, he's looking at you as if he'd like you for dinner.'

'Yuk, dirty little creep.'

'Got to go,' Blossom said suddenly, wanting to be out of the pub and by herself.

'Not seeing the fancy man, are we?' There was a smudge of envy in Bev's jokey voice.

'No.'

'When are you?'

'Wednesday.' Blossom's face suddenly looked a little lost.

'See, what did I tell ya? In love and miserable. Soon you'll be telling us you're getting married.'

'Not unless I can have a dress like Princess Di had!'

Bev and Tracy exchanged glances; they had that uneasy feeling that Blossom was no longer quite with them any more; that she was removed from their immediate world, from anything outside her own emotions.

'See you later, Bev. Try not to wake me up, won't you?'

'Oh, I'll just come in wearing me chain mail tonight. O.K.?' Then she turned to Tracy, 'Stay a bit Trace, now that Blossom's deserting us.'

And to Bev, watching Blossom's absorbed and secret face, it felt like that.

'O.K. I'll get us another drink. See you tomorrow at work, Bloss.' Tracy was quicker to forgive.

Bev sat looking thoughtfully into her empty glass; she'd have to keep an eye on Blossom all right, not let her get too wrapped up in this bloke. If you did that, it was fatal, you could lose your girlfriends before you knew it and life was a bad business without girlfriends. The men, they always pushed off in the end and left you with nothing and if you'd neglected your friends that was it. There were things Blossom wasn't telling, she was certain of it, and there must be a reason for that; there must be something a bit odd about this bloke if she couldn't talk about him openly. But she'd look after Bloss – she sort of needed it, she could be such an innocent.

Blossom walked down Kensington High Street to catch her bus. Her head was down and she was thinking of her beautiful pink dress. She wished she could just hold it for a minute. She felt a little afraid. She'd left the dress at Harold's: she couldn't take it to her budgie cage, nor home – it wouldn't stand up to questioning. It made her feel a bit deceitful; her life wasn't so simple now. But Harold had understood so well, he'd said, 'Well, think of it waiting here for you to come back to.' She'd hugged him then; he seemed to know just how to make her feel better.

She thought how Bev's face would go all thin if she saw that dress. Bev had a passion for what she called whoopee frocks – little cheap concoctions of mock-silk, or harsh satin, run up by careless machinists so that the seams went, the ruching drooped, the shoulder straps fell off and the cloth soon lost its enticing gleam. The pink dress couldn't even be *thought* of as a whoopee frock – it was a creation, a gown, something perfect in every one of its stitches and finishings. Then she remembered all the laughs and fun that she and Bev had had buying whoopee frocks before . . . before.

Before the Pink Dress.

She felt a little sad. Then cold. She turned and ran quickly down a side street full of trees until she found a telephone box. She went in quickly. She dialled the numbers and she heard his voice, low, mellow, dear to her already.

'Harold?'

'Yes.'

'It's me, it's Blossom.'

'Blossom!' His voice was in the box beside her, she could see his lovely grin lighting up that sombre face, she could feel his hands on her.

'I just, I just wanted to say thankyou for the weekend, for the lovely dress,' she stammered a little, then finally managed to say, 'for looking after me so well, making me feel so – so sort of wonderful.'

'Blossom, you *are* wonderful.' Then after a little silence he asked, 'I didn't know you knew my number?'

'Course I did, I learnt it by heart.' A space, in which she hesitated again. 'Harold?'

'Yes.'

'Harold, I love you.'

His eyes brimmed with tears and he didn't check them as they flowed down his face.

'Harold? Are you still there?'

'Yes.'

'Well, say you love me then!' She laughed, that lovely clear, uncomplicated sound.

'I love you, Blossom.'

'Good, see you tomorrow then. I'll walk to your place, shall I? Six-thirty?'

'As soon as you can.' He felt he would die a little until the moment he could see her again, and the cliché of it didn't bother him – it made him feel, at last, united with the world and common humanity.

His hand shuddered as he replaced the receiver. Then his face broke wide open into a hot excited laugh, his eyes closed for an instant and the sweetest relief filled his entire body, making him feel whole again.

Twenty-three

Harold was pulling dead heads off the marguerites as he stood by the window watching for her. His face was warm and happy. She came around the corner and began to walk in a brisk flowing way down the cobbled street. All of his attention was focused entirely on Blossom, on her movements, on the beautiful fuchsia dress – a wild, wicked splash of colour grabbing all the last of the sun's brilliance. The dress was short with a soft full skirt, and he could see her knees and quick golden gleams of her thighs as the wind flapped the cloth about. A couple of garage mechanics closing up for the night looked up at her in silent admiration, but she didn't notice them, and Harold didn't notice them. He could only anticipate the moment that she would knock on the door, and he would tear down the stairs and let her in.

He ran down the steep narrow staircase so fast that he nearly broke his neck. He opened the door to see her standing there with a punnet full of the fattest, reddest, shiniest cherries he'd ever seen. She walked in and put the punnet down. He appeared to have lost the use of his limbs. She put her arms around him and just held him still a moment.

'Look,' she took the punnet off the windowsill, 'aren't they beautiful?' She presented the cherries.

'I love cherries best of all,' he said, marvelling at the way she surrounded herself with the brightest colours without them ever striking a gaudy note. The colour of the dress was so vivid it seemed to hurt his eyes and yet her skin against it was so pure and creamy that the effect was exactly right – she had an ability to wear only what suited her.

'Can I come in then?'

'Of course, of course.' He backed away, nearly losing his

balance against the heel of the stairs. 'Whoever designed these bloody stairs ought to be shot,' he said, turning to lead her into the sitting room.

'Give us a glass of water, Harold, I'm dying of thirst.' Seed pearls of perspiration gleamed above her top lip. She sat down on his chair and stretched out her long legs, flipping off her flat leather pumps.

'Don't toes look awful,' she said, turning up her nose, 'when they're not painted?'

'They don't look awful to me,' he said. 'I've seldom seen such a nice pair of pinkies.'

'Pinkies!' she giggled and the child's teeth sparkled. 'Your mum must've called them that. I bet you were a gorgeous little boy.'

A cloud passed over the clear surface of his face and was gone.

'Oh I was,' he said brightly.

'You don't have sisters or brothers, do you?'

'No.' He left to get her water for her.

When he came back, she took a long swallow of the water and then said, 'It's a shame, you not having a brother or sister. I can't imagine myself ever being without Rosina.'

'Rosina?'

'Yeh, my sister. My mum got carried away with flowers, as you can tell.' She smiled fondly, 'Rosina was always there – she used to carry me around on her hip, pick me up when I fell over, I was ever such a fat little baby, you know. Rosina was a proper little mum to me, so they say.'

'Are you still close to her?'

'Oh yeah, but we fight as well. She's stupid with blokes, lets them mess her around.' She thought a bit, tilted her head at Harold and said, 'But weren't you lonely then as a kid, all on your own?' She drank the water down and he watched her long lazy neck tremble.

'No,' he said, 'no, I wasn't.' He took her glass, 'You sure you don't want a proper drink?'

She shook her head, 'No, that was lovely – ice and everything.' She let the ice blocks collide against the sides of the glass, and then tipped up the glass and let one block fall into her mouth, where she rolled it about until she could crunch it into pieces.

He sat down beside her and asked with a wonderful smile, 'Where shall I take you tonight?' He had thought up various treats: a superb restaurant in Richmond, an intimate French one in Soho – but it was too hot. He'd even got a chilled lobster and champagne in the fridge. She said she was coming round to champagne so he'd bought a couple of cases.

But Blossom shrugged and said, lazily, 'Oh, I don't know.' She took a small bottle of scarlet nail polish out of her handbag and held it a moment against her dress.

'It matches all right, doesn't it, Harold?' He loved this, it felt so domestic, so familiar.

'Yes, it's a bit darker, which is fine.' You'd think he'd been consulted about nail polish all his life.

She moved to the floor and sat down, hoisting up the skirt of her dress, then brought up her knees, letting them fall open as she leaned forward to paint her toenails.

'I thought,' he said, watching her thighs with a hard constriction in his groin, 'I thought we might go to a restaurant in Holland Park, since it's so humid and hot. It'll be cooler than eating inside and the food's good.'

'Yeh?' She concentrated on her toes, the little brush making thin red strokes. When she'd finished painting the toes of her left foot, she looked up and said, 'I feel a bit bad, guilty I suppose, with you sometimes, Harold.'

'What about?' He was quite startled.

'You taking me to expensive places all the time. It makes me feel bad.'

'But why?'

'Because other people don't have the chance. My mum, she's probably never been *near* a lovely restaurant like the one you took me to, never eaten food like you cook or drunk out of a thin glass.'

'You shouldn't feel guilty about things like that,' he said firmly, 'they're not important.'

'But money *is* important,' she said, frowning, 'if you don't have it it's the most important thing in the world.' A little flush had touched up her cheekbones.

'But if you do, you shouldn't consider it, it's to be spent, that's all, on what you like best, on who you like best.' He felt like giving her all his money – for her mum, and her out-of-work dad, for Rosina's fatherless baby – the lot, just handing it over. Particularly if it was likely to cause tension between them.

She bent to do her other toenails and said quietly, 'But I can't spend money on you. I can't return things.' Then he understood her difficulty and saw that it was more complicated than he'd imagined.

'But why should you return things?' he said carefully. 'In any case, you bring me orchids, and pots of jam, and cherries, lovely things like that.'

She ignored this and continued stubbornly, 'It'll make me feel unequal. I'd like to be able to take *you* to dinner.'

He smiled with pleasure and surprise, 'Are you a feminist, Blossom?'

'No,' she said, 'no, I'm not, or at least I don't know if I am or not. I just don't like things to be one-sided. Money makes things one-sided.'

'Perhaps you don't want to feel beholden to me?' he said with a trace of anxiety. 'But Blossom, I do what little I have done because I care for you, I love you, I *want* to look after you and give you things you can't give yourself. At least not yet. It gives me the greatest pleasure to do it.'

'Yes,' she said with a steely smile, 'not *yet*.'

'Well,' he said lightly, 'when you're a rich and famous *couturière*, you can take me driving in your Rolls-Royce.'

She laughed and he thought she would forget the subject, but she stretched her arms behind her on the carpet, looked him straight in the eye and said, 'You've never been unemployed, Harold, have you?'

'No.'

'Then you don't know what it's like – real worry about money. It changes everything. It changes people.'

His brow drew in and he found himself taking careful note of her in a very different way from before. 'No,' he said thoughtfully, 'I've never really thought about what it means, how it affects people.' He was ashamed, for the first time, of the casualness of his regard for money, of the easiness of his life – the way he had gained material security without it ever hurting.

'That's because you've never had to,' she said sharply – angry at him for her father's sake, for her deprived and exhausted mother's sake, for her own sake. 'You've always been properly educated, so when you came to look for a job it was bound to be a yes, not a no. Do you know what it feels like to have people saying no to you, keep sending you away week by week?' Her voice now wobbled like a jelly.

He put out his hand to lift her chin and saw a large tear on her cheek. 'Blossom,' he said tenderly, wiping the tear away, 'don't be angry with me. I'm sorry for your dad, really I am, I can tell how much you care about him.'

She buried her face in his neck and wailed softly, 'I just hate – not to be able to help him. To watch him get snappy at my mum, not talk, not go out, get bitter and twisted inside. He's such a sweet man and now the worst thing is when he just sits there, like someone very old. And I can't help him at all.' It was like the despair of someone watching a loved one growing daily more ill and weak.

'I know,' she said, sitting up and wiping her tears away, 'I know that people can't imagine what they haven't lived.' She wanted to exonerate him from his happy ignorance and there was a sombre wisdom in her face as she reached for the bottle of nail polish to give her toenails their second coat. Then her features rounded again and she smiled at him brightly and demanded, 'Where are those cherries?' She kissed him quickly on the chin.

'I'll get them.' It hurt him to leave her just to walk across the room to fetch the cherries. He put them down next to her and said, 'Shall I paint your toes so you can eat them?'

'No,' she said, 'I've got a better idea: I'll paint my toes and you can feed me.'

He popped the dark red globes in her mouth and watched as her teeth tugged each cherry from its stem. In minutes the cherries with their taut shiny skin and scarlet juice had stained her lips and tongue. He almost forgot to eat any himself watching her. He began to decorate each of her toes with the double-corded cherries; he hung them up around her ears like lanterns. He had to kiss her, but strangely, the dark staining of her mouth did not penetrate his lips, while hers grew redder and sweeter by the minute.

'Harold,' she said, looking down at him, her hand propping up her chin. 'I don't think we should go to that restaurant, we should go to the pictures. It's not so hot now.'

He laughed, liking the way she knew exactly what she wanted.

'Yes, let's,' he said. He never went to the pictures. He didn't mind eating alone, it bothered him not at all to sit in a restaurant by himself and read a good book, but he couldn't abide the idea of queueing alone, or sitting in the dark alone watching a film. But being alone now seemed a very distant idea.

'There's a French film near by,' she said. 'It's very rude so you'll like it.' She stood up and looked at her bright toes, 'Nice, aren't they, Harold?'

'Lovely,' he said and kissed them.

She picked up her bag and put on her shoes. 'Then, when we come back,' she said sweetly, 'I'll make you bacon and eggs. I know how to do that at least.'

'I'd like that,' he said, though he hardly ever ate fried food, 'I can tell you're determined to look after me tonight.'

'Yes,' she said, putting her arms around him, 'I am, because, Harold,' she kissed him softly, 'you're the goodest one I've ever known.' The blue eyes rippled as she looked up at him.

'It's you who make me that way,' he said, and felt with a quickening of fear that he'd never really existed before this moment, this woman, and that as soon as she was gone he became a void again, a shadow wandering through a house, living a life that could only echo without her.

Twenty-four

Harold was sitting in front of his drawing board finishing the first draft of some plans for the Alexander kitchen. It was the best part, the beginning, when he could put down in a pure form what ought to be done. Later it would be compromised by taste less good than his and by financial considerations. Unless he was lucky – sometimes he was, very lucky; there were a few gems nestling inside unexpected addresses in Fulham, Kensington and Chelsea where no such compromises had taken place.

And yet, today as he worked, he felt curiously detached from it all. He couldn't settle; he kept walking to the window where he had seen her walk in the high-throated fuchsia dress, her hair poured around her face like rain. But the mews was empty and the sky a mottled grey. He wanted the sun to shine because it was Friday and she was coming – it was the weekend; he was taking her away.

It had seemed so reasonable to say, 'Come with me to Rye, I'd like you to see where I was brought up. It's by the sea.' How her face had lit up when he'd said the sea, suddenly filling with depth and sparkle. But of course it wasn't as simple as that. He never returned to the past; it was an uncharted place of lost maps and forgotten landmarks. And yet here he was, willing her into a secret side of himself, trying to take her to a place he'd never properly inhabited himself.

It was lunchtime. He'd made the decision not to go round and check up on Max and had telephoned the builder to say so. Max was one of those invaluable men who could make other men work – by jollying and threatening, bullying and teasing. He was also a congenital liar, though he preferred to see himself as an optimist. He liked to promise that a job would be done when he'd like it to be done. It never was, and he and Harold had achieved a good working relationship only because Harold never listened to Max's promises. He worked out the schedules himself and those were the dates he told the clients. Max thought this just fine, it saved him rows, and his easygoing West Indian nature hated unpleasantness. Harold had never had a row in his life. He circumvented trouble of any kind.

Max was surprised when Harold rang to say he wasn't coming. The conversion was getting close to completion; the plastering was done and Harold would always check this. But then, Harold had not been himself lately. It would never occur to Max to ask him why; Harold was not a man you could intrude upon, and he and Max had never even had a drink in a pub together. And yet, curiously, this distance never seemed to cause offence; there was a kindness and generosity in Harold that made people accept him the way he was.

Harold left the window and looked around his study. It was a bright airy room with dove-grey walls and a white ceiling. The curtains and carpet were a very pale grey-blue. His drawing board was close to the window, and in the other corner a large roll-top desk gave dignity to an otherwise modern room. On glass shelves a collection of beautifully feminine pots and bowls was arranged, each one unique, hand-thrown – and priceless porcelain with delicate carvings and muted colours. Standing out among these was a Japanese ceramic pot, one he loved especially because it was not round like the Chinese pots his father had once collected so avidly. This was interestingly asymmetrical, showing what he felt was the Japanese respect and understanding of the wonderful imperfections of natural things. Like the slightly crumpled aspect of Blossom's right ear which he loved more dearly than its perfect sister.

Because he was unsettled, not merely restless, he went down to the kitchen. Food would comfort him; it had a curious therapeutic effect on his mind as well as his body. If he was hungry he became very unhappy and then the performance of preparing, cooking and eating a meal would restore him and give him security. He took a glistening red mullet out of the fridge and laid it on a slab of marble. From a long rack of knives, each one having a specific purpose and used for no other, he selected a filleting knife. He found himself thinking of a Japanese friend of his who'd taught him how to ritually prepare a fish in such a way that when it was cut and the backbone removed, the fish fitted together again as if it were perfect and whole – uncut. Harold did this now, quickly, expertly, the knife slipping through the red mullet's flesh to the bone, separating one from the other so meticulously that when the backbone was put to one side, the tail came back against the body, the head nestled against the fins and no knife mark showed. He liked the silkiness of the fish against his hand and the precision of the knife as it slid through the flesh, and it gave him a pleasant satisfaction to be able to execute this faultlessly.

While the fish was grilling and he sliced cucumbers and chopped dill, Harold remembered how much he'd once admired the traditional Japanese way of life. His obsession had started with Mishima. The all-embracing nature of Japanese traditions, the Buddhist self-control and discipline, the high placing of honour and courtesy, and the way gentleness was inseparable from violence had appealed to him for years. He had felt, and still did feel, that he understood the nobility and the grotesque nature of hara-kiri, the pure idealism of a way of life that could survive intact in industrial Japan. He was intrigued by the extremes of life and emotion, but had never before dared to enter that magic and dangerous circle. Having once done so, he felt he would be compelled to the same excesses.

He began to eat his fish; the flesh was silky pink, cooked to perfection. He cut it tenderly, separating it into neat, small shapes. Slowly as he ate, he found that a deep feeling of well-being and peace came over him. He had been sitting very upright, his back not touching the chair. Now, as he continued to eat, his eyes became softer and less fixed and his arms fell forward in a relaxed way on to the table. He had the warm fulfilled look of a man who has been soothed and comforted by sex; and, in fact, his feelings at that moment were very close to the ones he felt after sleeping with Blossom.

As he sat a little longer in the dining room – he never ate in the kitchen – he drank a glass of wine and began to remember Blossom that first night of the banquet – how she had grown rosy in the pink dress, how he had entered her sweet body there on the carpet, like a root finding its true earth. He was consumed by a passion so real that he could actually smell her, feel and taste her skin against his lips. The desire was so sharp in him that it made him shudder violently.

Then it passed, like the pang of pain he sometimes felt waking, having just broken a dream. His watch announced that there were only four hours to be endured before he could collect her from outside Marks and Spencer. He had a lot to do, he had to pack for a start. His decision to take her to Rye had been made in the middle of a long night, prompted by half-formed dreams and mixed recollections. He knew that the journey back would be vital to him, that the days that he and Blossom spent alone together there would determine their future. He had to test it, the past against the present, and see if it would hold or flounder. He had to know whether she was really the woman he'd idealized for so long, or merely a sad mockery of his loneliness and longing.

Twenty-five

Blossom came walking out of the doors of Marks and Spencer the way light streams through a window. Harold was parked close to the bus-stop and did not get out of his car until the bevy of girls had leapt on to the bus, laughing at those who'd arrived too late and missed it. Being close to these clean-faced girls was a real pleasure for him, because they and this shop were so entirely bound up in his love for Blossom. Then she saw him and came running forward. A little behind her a dark-haired girl hung back shyly, but Blossom turned and yanked her forward by the hand.

'This is Bev, Harold,' she said proudly as he walked towards them. And Bev smiled nervously, her rosebud mouth retracting in the wide face.

'Hello Bev, I've heard a lot about you.' Bev relaxed. She thought he was rather dishy and sort of nice the way he talked and the way his eyes seemed to look inside you and be pleased by what they saw.

'Here, Blossom, let me take your suitcase,' Harold said. She handed it over obediently and he put it in the back seat of the car. Bev moved over to Blossom and hissed in her ear, 'It's a Peugeot, you idiot, that's a ruddy Peugeot!'

Blossom laughed and shrugged slightly; Harold looked at her so she felt bound to explain, 'It's just that I didn't know what kind of car you had, you see, Bev likes to know these things.'

'Oh I see.' He looked at Blossom and said, 'Shall we have a drink with Bev before we go?'

'Oh no,' Bev said, 'you must get off, it'll get dark.'

'Not for hours,' Blossom laughed, turning to wave at Stella, who was walking quickly in the direction of the tube station.

'It's a long way,' Bev said like a mother.

'We could just go round the corner,' Harold suggested, but not wanting to.

'No, I must be off,' Bev said, and moved backwards so that she and Blossom stood side by side. Harold thought there was something wonderful and quite remarkable about the polarity of their looks. It was a little like putting an aubergine beside a lily – the effect was fascinating and strange.

Blossom moved to the car with a 'Well if you're sure, Bev,' and he opened the door for her; she was still talking to Bev as she got in, folding the vivid blue dress around her thighs.

'Good-bye Bev, it was nice to meet you,' Harold said.

'You too,' she said shortly, suddenly not wanting Blossom to go with him.

When they were both in the car, Bev smiled and waved, but there was something about her of the child left behind when the others have gone to the seaside. Impulsively, Blossom opened her door, rushed out and gave Bev a random kiss, which landed on her ear.

'I'll bring you a stick of rock back,' she promised.

'It's not really that kind of seaside,' Harold said when she was back in again and the car moved off. Blossom's arm waved wildly at Bev, who now turned and walked away.

'Poor Bev,' Blossom said, 'the Brute's being horrible again. Keeps chasing after some girl at the club and pretending he's going round to her house to see her brother.'

'Why does she put up with him?' Harold asked, sliding on his driving gloves. 'She's pretty enough to find someone else.'

'You think she's pretty do you, Harold?'

'Oh yes, in a way.'

'Me, too. I don't know why she sticks with him really, well perhaps I do. She loves him, you see,' Blossom added simply, sniffing loudly in the way he found so touching. 'She pretends she's just after a good time, but really she loves him. Or she wouldn't get so angry – you only get angry like that when you're hurt.' She sniffed again, 'He's no good though and he won't change.' He thought how emphatic she could be, so sure of herself and her opinions.

'Was your last boyfriend like that?' he asked, a sexual curiosity surfacing and with it an unpleasant smart of jealousy.

'No,' Blossom said, 'he wasn't bad to me, nothing like that, he was just boring, he wasn't going anywhere.' Then she turned to him eagerly, 'And where are *we* going, Harold, you haven't said exactly.' This had made it quite easy with Bev, she could honestly say it was all a surprise.

'To Sussex,' he said, smiling broadly.

'I know *that*! But *where*?'

'Oh a lovely place,' he said. 'You must learn to anticipate things, not gobble them all up at once.' To lessen the didactic note, he leaned across and kissed her. 'When you wake up in the morning you might hear mermaids singing.'

She liked him when he was like this – like a magician who could pull wonderful surprises out of the air.

'I'm so excited,' she said, lifting her shoulders and clenching her hands together. There was great security for him in the fact that she couldn't be disappointed; there was no part of her that was jaded or blasé; her expectations, her palate, like her kisses, were as clean as a child's. A more sophisticated woman would be harder to enchant, but with her everything was so new, so untried, that she could respond to a particular atmosphere or a beautiful meal with such naïve and total pleasure.

She talked to him about her day as he drove and he gave a version of his so that it sounded industrious. She was a great believer in hard work. But by the time they reached the motor-way she'd grown quiet and was watching the countryside speed by, saying very little. He felt utterly comfortable with this silence, and was glad of it. And because he loved her so much he imagined that she thought the same thoughts that he did; he could almost believe that they had become the same person.

'Harold,' she said suddenly, turning to him, 'I'm starving.'

'I knew you would be,' he laughed, 'but I deliberately

stopped myself bringing a tuck box along for you. You'll have to wait because we're having dinner when we get there.'

'Yes mum,' she said with mock humility.

'On the other hand, you could have a barley sugar,' he indicated the glove compartment.

She took three, gave one to him and put the other two in her mouth and then let them crash about noisily against her teeth.

'I wonder if ostriches make a din like that when they're eating stones?' he said.

'They don't suck 'em even, they just swallow them, very quietly,' she said with authority. Then her attention was drawn to the countryside and she said, 'Hey, Harold, this is a nice bit, it looks like Holland or something.'

'That's an oasthouse.'

'And look at those lovely little lambs, the way they jump about as if they've got springs in their legs.'

'Hm, delicious,' he said, 'with mint sauce and new potatoes, nothing better.'

'Oh, you're a beast,' she said, 'poor little bleeders, they'll soon be down someone's gullet without you planning a meal around them.'

'My gullet, I hope,' he said, ducking her hand that was about to whap him on the arm.

'I'm going to have a snooze,' she announced, 'just for ten minutes.'

'Carry on then,' he said happily, watching her settle her golden head against the brown seat cover.

In a few minutes he could tell by her breathing that she was asleep. He tucked a stray curl tenderly behind her ear so that he could see the round curve of her cheek, and then, impulsively, bent and kissed it with the greatest affection. A feeling of warmth and trust surfaced in him and he loved her all the more deeply for rekindling such human emotions within him.

Twenty-six

He was watching Blossom as she slept with a painful tenderness. It reminded him of the times he had walked into his mother's bedroom on dusky early mornings, wanting to curl himself into her soft warm arms, but stopped, because she was sleeping and he couldn't bear to shatter such peacefulness in her. Her waking hours were less calm. He desperately wanted Blossom to wake up: she had gone too far from him in sleep; he wanted the reassurance of her smile to banish these encroaching thoughts of his mother.

It was getting dark and the sky had a heaviness that threatened rain. The marshes began, the land lying flat and lifeless with a beauty only discernible to those who love bleakness and great sweeps of sky which a landscape propped by hills and valleys lacks. He felt he knew this road through the marshes as he knew the lines of his own body. But when he reached a particular curve in the road, it brought back a terrible memory so deeply entrenched in his mind that to remember it winded him: a car swerving, brakes, the car reeling, glass shattering, a head flung forward, a lock of blonde hair clotting with blood. Grief axed him. The car swerved under his hands, he felt the wheels spin. Blossom awoke with a sharp cry. He skidded to a halt beside the narrow road, up on the grass. He was sweating, his hands shaking and his face so white that Blossom was terrified.

'What is it, Harold?' She reached out for him. But he had opened his door, and got out shakily. She did so too and ran around to him, her face tense. 'Oh Harold, what happened?' She was almost tearful, she couldn't bear the unhappiness in his face.

He righted himself with chilling expertise. 'I'm so sorry. Are you all right, Blossom?' He put his arm around her and there was no tremble in him.

'Yes, I'm fine, just got a fright. But what happened, Harold?' Her little face with its exquisite mouth was unbearably beautiful to him as he saw its distress.

'Nothing, it was nothing.' He led her quickly back to her side of the car and helped her in, then drove off.

When they were a little way along the road, he felt he had to say something to her; he sensed that she felt mystified and excluded, so he said, 'There was a hedgehog on the road, a dead one. I can't bear running over them. I'm sorry to make such a fuss about it.' The face he turned to her was quite relaxed, the grief all smoothed away.

She settled down in her seat, instantly reassured and said, 'It's horrible, I know, all squashed like that. Don't think about it, Harold.' She touched his knee softly.

But as he drove on he was filled with a sickness that he was so calm in this lying, this hiding of his true face from her; it would be so easy for him to slip back into alienation. He wanted with all his heart to return to those trusting feelings he'd felt a moment before when she first fell asleep.

'Harold?' she asked, 'Are we nearly there?'

'Oh yes, my darling, we are, nearly there.'

Tears, old unshed tears, rose up and it took all his concentration to force them back.

Twenty-seven

'Is this it?' Blossom peered out of a rainy windscreen at a very old building. 'Is this where we're staying, Harold?' Then she saw the sign.

'But Harold – it's a hotel!' Her voice flopped.

'Where did you think we would be staying?' he asked calmly, and she thought how strange it was that his voice never rose in anger or impatience.

'I don't know.' She was a little sulky.

For some reason she'd imagined he'd be taking her to his parents' home; now the mystery of so much of his life baffled her. She began to wonder what she really did know about him; he was so private, so inaccessible in so many ways. She turned her face away from him and watched the drops of water trickling down the glass; she could just make out her own face and she didn't like the expression on it.

He leaned towards her gently, 'It's all right, my sweet, it's a beautiful old hotel. I chose it specially for you. It was built at the time of Elizabeth the First.'

'I don't need to know its history and architecture,' she said grumpily, her lips pouting.

He was wounded by her tone and said carefully, 'What is it, Blossom, what's the matter?'

'Nothing.'

'There must be, I've never seen you like this.'

'That's because you don't know me that well.'

'I know you that well, Blossom, and I suggest you tell me what's the matter.'

'I can't,' she said sadly.

'Of course you can, it's only me.'

'I'm just embarrassed,' she said forlornly and he knew

that had she been standing her feet would have toppled sideways.

He took her hand. 'Come on Blossom, what is it? Everything can be solved you know.'

'Can it?' Her face lifted, full of confidence in him, and immediately he believed what he'd just said.

'Harold,' she said quietly, 'I can't go in there.'

'Why ever not?'

'I just can't.' She wiped her finger under her nose. She sniffed and wriggled in her seat.

'Blossom, you're being dotty, now out with it and tell me this minute.'

'Harold,' she said in a small whisper, 'they'll know we're not married in there.' He restrained himself from laughing out loud.

'Oh Blossom,' he began, startled by her lack of sophistication, 'no one will . . .'

'Oh it might not matter to you,' she said sharply, 'perhaps you've done it a million times, but I haven't.' She'd actually never stayed in a hotel in her entire life – bed and breakfasts were what her mum and dad liked on their holidays. And this hotel was so formidable, and Harold so strange.

'I've never done it before,' he said.

'But you don't understand,' she said dismally, knowing that she just could not walk in there and feel happy.

'Oh yes I do,' he said, producing from his pocket a plush little box which snapped open to reveal, perched on its black velvet hillock, a circle of gold inlaid with tiny pearls. 'Here is something to adorn your married finger, so it isn't naked and ashamed.' His voice, though sometimes mocking, was never cruel.

He handed it to her and watched the pleasure fill her face until it looked in danger of overflowing.

'We'll put it on and then no one will know,' he said, slipping it on to her finger.

'Oh Harold,' she whispered.

'I didn't get a plain gold ring, in case you might be super-stitious about that,' he said, 'but it's pretty, isn't it, and very old.' He was deliberately matter-of-fact, making little of his ability to be always one step ahead of any doubt or mishap that might crush her.

She rested her head on his shoulder a minute and said, 'Oh, Harold, you are *so* good to me.' Then she lifted her head and kissed him passionately on the mouth again and again.

'Shall we go in then?' he asked, lifting her hand to his mouth and kissing it. 'Will you come with me now?' He smiled tenderly, 'Now that you're my bride?'

No man, he thought, watching her dance around to his side of the car and embrace him, no man had a more willing and beautiful bride. No man in the world was better blessed. She looked up at him and laughed like a wayward child; she danced round him in a ring; she grabbed him by the arms and whirled in the rain with him; she threw herself at him and kissed him again besottedly. She even tried to carry the suit-cases in for him; she wanted to be his slave, to walk behind him, to wait on him hand and foot, to adore him to the grave.

'Give me those suitcases, before you fall in that puddle,' he said, snatching them from her, and walking fast to the hotel entrance.

Just before they reached the door, she ran up beside him and said breathlessly, 'I feel as if we are, we really are married. Oh Harold, you are such a love and I love you so.' She pushed her wet face into his throat so that the suitcases tumbled down the stone stairs. He enfolded her in his arms and held her so tightly that she lost her breath for a moment and seemed almost to faint.

When she had recovered, she could walk into the elegant sixteenth-century hotel like a woman who was bred to such grace and dignity; and who, with her rain-spangled hair and damp dazzling face, could outshine all the impeccable beauties of the world.

Twenty-eight

Oh Blossom, my bride, it was just as you said, it was as if we were really married. And all I have done, or tried to do, is to make us more so, only more so. She shall be of my flesh and I shall be of hers. One flesh, one heart, one soul. Oh my Blossom, I would never hurt you. We are most truly married as the world in its normality will never tolerate. You are my flesh and I am yours. For always.

It was her flesh that I loved so, that I paid homage to in the only way left to me. It was a celebration of that love. I took her within me, with the deepest reverence, like a communion wafer I placed her upon my tongue. And she became me. We became one. Oh Blossom, there is no grief like the grief of loss, no sorrow like the loss of love. No agony like the love of you. Oh Blossom.

Twenty-nine

'Oh Harold, it's so wonderful here. What shall I eat?'

'Whatever you like, my darling.'

'But you must tell me, I can't decide, it's all so yummy.'

'Why not start with the salmon mousse?'

She leant towards him and breathed, 'Do you think these people are dressed so beautifully because they know we are married?'

'Definitely, they knew we were coming.'

'I'll have the duck afterwards, with lots of roast potatoes and all the vegetables and a salad as well.' She gave a little groan of delight, 'Oh Harold, *look* what lovely puddings they have.'

'Well, I'm sure you'll have room for everything.'

He smiled at her as she sat pulling apart her bread roll. She was wearing a black dress with a square throat and tight bodice. ('I thought a little black dress would be swanky,' she'd said, 'though I've had it for ever.') Just the very slightest swell of her breasts showed at the neckline. She wore the pearls; they cascaded down her dress. She had stood at the mirror and coiled them into two ropes: 'No, too old-fogeyish; one loop? No, they'll drip in my soup.' In the end she settled for a knot that caught the pearls softly between her breasts.

'Harold,' she said brightly, 'now that we're here, you can tell me lots of stories about when you were little, can't you? You know all about me and Ros and mum and dad, but you don't say about you. I want to know what you were like. You know, sometimes you seem full of secrets.'

'I suppose I never learnt to talk about myself much, people so much prefer to talk about themselves in any case.' He flipped out his napkin.

'But you feel left out if you're only talking about yourself, you don't feel cosy with the other person if they're just listening.'

'Hm, I know what you mean. It is a fault.' He rearranged the butter so she could reach it easily.

'Oh, not a fault,' she kissed him quickly, 'just a shyness probably.'

Harold was good at stories; he'd always got his essays in the school magazine and was good at amusing people with little anecdotes, based on the truth but well embellished, or carefully edited to be fit for general consumption.

'Well,' he said, as she reached across and whipped his bread roll, 'funny you should say that really. My father and mother used to bring me here for Sunday lunch sometimes. It was very good: roast beef and yorkshire puddings and homemade apple pie. We used to sit by those windows there.'

She sat and listened to the picture he presented of happy family outings, and of how his father, the doctor, had taught him how to make wonderful darts and intricate shapes with the starched napkins. While he talked, her eyes took in the long room with its white tablecloths, deep stone fireplaces and walls with linenfold panelling. Inside the fireplaces low tables with silver dishes gleamed and vases of tall red gladioli lit up the corners of the room like fires. She thought it all quite lovely, like one of those grand country houses you had to pay to look at. She raised her neck and her quivering throat with its baby flesh made his blood roar so much that he gave up talking and just watched her. Then bent over and kissed her throat. She barely noticed because her salmon mousse was at last being escorted down to her by the waiter.

When she was concentrating on her duck and he was eating some rather indifferent trout, he told her stories about his schooldays – odd stories that made him seem vulnerable and quirky even – not a boy to play rugger, beat up new boys in the lavatories or tell crude stories about sex.

'I wasn't a great success at school,' he said with a grin, 'I was bookish and boring and I think I wasn't cruel enough to be really popular. Though once, when I was new, they pushed me too far, trying to make me lose my temper, because none of them believed I couldn't be forced to break.'

'Did they make you lose your temper?'

'No.' He hesitated and she watched his face close. 'But I was forced to bend the bugger's arm until he screamed for mercy. I broke it as a matter of fact,' he added wryly.

'Ugh,' she said, not eating now, 'aren't boys horrible and cruel.'

'Children are cruel,' he said quietly, 'and the cruellest adults are children who have never grown up.'

'Hitler must have been like that,' she said pensively. Then she added with a squeeze of his arm, 'But I would have loved you, Harold, even then, even when you broke that boy's arm. I would have still married you.'

'No, you wouldn't. I was revolting.'

'You couldn't have been, Harold, you were never revolting,' she said, her eyes basking like a blue sea.

And from that moment it was as if her view of him became history, and all the rest, the true past, ceased to exist.

Eating exhausted Blossom because she did it with complete dedication and single-mindedness. Afterwards a listlessness settled over her features. It caused an unbearable sense of tension in Harold which made his voice quick and harsh, 'Shall we go for a walk, or would you rather go to bed?'

'To bed,' she whispered, taking his hand under the table-cloth, 'right now.'

As they walked out of the dining room, an elderly couple watched them and smiled reminiscently at one another.

They walked slowly down narrow low corridors ('Mrs Tittlemouse should live here,' she said) with white and black everywhere, red carpeting, floors that ran downhill and then up again entirely at their own whim; oak chests, oil paintings on the walls and a lovely smell of age and dust.

'Must be riddled with woodworm,' he said with disgust, woodworm and dry rot being his pet hates.

A homely chair was set in a nook and she flopped into it as he searched for the key outside their bedroom door. He looked sideways at her as he applied the key to the lock.

When she entered the room she gasped again as she had done the first time she saw the Elizabethan bedchamber with its panelled walls and door, the white brocade chair, the voluptuous cream hangings of the four-poster bed, the fireplace with a vase of scarlet roses and the soft light coming through diamond-shaped lead windows.

She turned to the fireplace and said softly, indicating the roses, 'Those weren't there when we came in?'

She bent down on her haunches and pushed her nose into them, turning a little towards him as he stood behind her. 'Did the hotel put them there, or,' her voice became husky, 'was it you?' She licked one of the petals and whispered, 'Oh, it was you, wasn't it, it was you?'

Her hand groped out behind her and, without turning from the roses, she grabbed his leg and squeezed it hard. With a voice thrumming with pleasure, she said, 'Thank you.' Then turned and buried her face in his trouser leg.

It was as if he knew, precisely, all the ways to please her, to make her feel cosseted and adored. And she succumbed to all these gentle snares with the same impulse that made it impossible for her to walk past a jeweller's shop without looking in, without aching to possess those feminine temptations.

She had got into bed, after turning the covers back carefully, not wanting to spoil the crisp cotton. Then she sat there, clean, fragrant and naked, her smooth legs stretched out, her hair fluffy as a soufflé.

'Oh hurry up, Harold, what are you doing?' Her body seemed to vibrate with excitement and happiness. 'It's wicked to be alone in a bed like this.'

'I'm about to call down and tell reception when we want

our morning tea – on this extraordinary contraption that looks like an old wireless.'

In the distance she could hear the thunder of a lavatory emptying, gushing and gurgling like a rickety machine about to explode, then very slowly refilling itself, until finally, with a deep sigh, it expired.

'We're not going to get much sleep here,' she said with a giggle, 'if that thing goes off all night.' She settled back on the pillows, looking over her pink nipples. 'And we'll have to be a bit quiet ourselves, too,' she whispered with a lewd smile, 'you can hear everything through these bleeding walls.'

He pulled the cord of the curtains so that they were drawn almost to the middle, but left enough of an opening for a chunk of the morning sun to get in.

'Well, I imagine people only come to places like this to fuck anyway,' he said thoughtfully, 'probably stuffed with honeymoon couples and new brides shouting out their appreciation.'

'Harold!' She looked faintly shocked.

He joined her in the fat springy bed, clicking off the white bedside light. The mattress seemed to have arms that enfolded them in a matronly embrace. The sheets were slippery-smooth and the plump pillows swallowed Blossom's small face and wild mop of curls. Relief flooded him at being close to her flesh again – relief and a peaceful feeling of having returned home. He held her gently and nuzzled into her neck, then raised his body on to hers and settled like a bird on a nest. She felt warm and protective of him, full of the desire to reassure him, to make him feel strong and secure in this private peace he had created for them both.

Soon he could feel, could almost hear, her taut flesh begin to sizzle beneath his. He kissed the corner of her parted mouth, her throat, the little line above her breasts where the tight bodice had cut into her. Her hands began to move with the same urgency as his. He buried his head in her stomach, kissed her belly, her thighs, the lovely knees and calves, whispering like a man paying homage, 'I love you, I love you, I love you.'

He slept and she lay awake watching a pool of moonlight spreading on the carpet. She kept looking at his face, so sad and defenceless in sleep, but she could not read it. In the darkness she felt a tremor of fear: he spun from such passion to such dependence. There was something hounding him, and at times she could only watch terrified, waiting for him to return to the peace she offered so openly in her arms.

But perhaps he will kill me, she thought, her eyes wide and strange, perhaps he will. And she was more exhilarated and terrified than at any time in her life. Perhaps he will kill me, perhaps he will have to. Because I can never leave him now, never. How can I leave him when he loves me so?

Thirty

She asked me one night in Rye about my first sexual experience, and told me laughingly about a boy called Norman who'd stroked her thighs and run his thumb into her when she was thirteen. It was so innocent and untortured. And there was a boy she'd loved so much she wanted to tidy his room and put all his Dinky cars in a big box, laid out carefully so he could find each one. And a boy who'd brought her some flowers when she was sick but was too embarrassed to give them to her, so sat with them in his lap until he left, by which time he'd broken all the stems. I had no innocent childhood reminiscences to swap with her, so I made up a few stories which she liked. But it saddened me to have to do so – I so envied that easy childhood, I felt sometimes that I wanted to steal it.

When I was a student, I realized that love seemed to have been scotched in me by my mother's desertion. I forgot love, I pushed it away; my work was all that mattered. I spent my hours feverishly working for exams which I passed brilliantly and was left feeling no sense of pleasure or achievement. I settled for bought pleasures. None of these girls were chosen with care. I watched their eyes in the street and read their message; I always waited for them to turn round and look back at me – that gave me the courage to follow them home. But they were simple girls, working girls. It's the working girl I admire – the ones with tough little faces and harsh make-up concealing soft yearning eyes. I've never touched one of those brisk, efficient secretaries with voices like electric typewriters and air-conditioned smiles. Working girls – girls conventional and coarse, wonderful and real.

Like my Blossom. But of course she was different, something set her apart. Not just her beauty – not just the sweetness in her that mingled with that tough insistence on something better. She was more than all that because I had made her so, my love transfigured her so that each day she became more exceptional. Perhaps she came to know it too, though originally her uniqueness was a complete mystery to her. Once she said: 'I don't know why you chose me, why me? You could have found someone much better.' She knew that she was chosen. But she also chose me, and she came to know that too, and perhaps even to know what she had chosen me for.

Blossom, and I, in those idyllic few days spent in Rye, discovered that the perfection of our physical harmony was only possible because of our spiritual unity. She understood me. We were the same – or so we came to believe. Our frenzy of possession could only be eased by a total consumption of one another – mind, flesh and soul. We grew dizzier with one another. Were you afraid, my darling, as I was, by the passion we felt for one another? The way our limbs locked and our flesh melted? Once I thought our insides had fused. You were more frightened than I. Much more. You soon learned that my sexual desperation was too much for even your generosity to ease; too great a burden for that sweet and golden body.

What frightened me most was the certainty that it was a time of the most perfect happiness, and we would try to return to it all our lives and never find it again.

Oh Blossom, it is only now that I can see that by taking you there I was trying, through you, to reincarnate my mother. I had rediscovered at the age of thirty-one all I'd had to forget with such anguish at the age of six. Six is so little an age. On this dreadful day, as I wait here alone and seem to hear your key in the lock, your voice calling me from upstairs, on this dreadful day I feel as little and as vulnerable to the recklessness of time as I was then.

The most extraordinary thing is that all the years in between – after my mother and before you – they dissolved. From that moment when she had gone to the moment I saw and chose you, the past vanished, because it was meaningless. Only you and my mother had reality. But in taking you, Blossom, in allowing you so deep within me, you and she became one, the love became the same love. She no longer haunted me because you had become her. And I knew I would never lose you as I had lost her. If I lost my life I would keep you; if you lost your life I would keep you. You were mine, Blossom, mine, you were *me*, and no poet could describe what I felt for you. It is too exhausting for me to try. And it cuts me to the very bone to think of this and know that my passion may be judged in other ways, by hearts less loving, less desperate than ours were during those most beautiful days in Rye.

Thirty-one

I lived in thee, and dreamed, and waked
Twice what I had been.

T. STURGE MOORE

Harold woke early the next morning. Blossom was curled up with her back to him, her backbones sharp as the spines on a sea-shell – those shells that are lined with pink satin and which echo the sea's breathing. She slept so soundly that even gentle biting did not wake her; she swatted intruders away with her long hands and slept on. She has the fingers of Persephone in Rossetti's painting, he thought, getting out of bed and opening the window to let the morning in.

There was a soft mist, a salty dampness that made him feel that the harbour had moved closer. A milk float bumped over the smooth round pebbles, and from the window he could see an old lady busy at a jigsaw puzzle. A dog barked, the postboy whistled as he trudged. Life was going on outside in the pale sunshine – but he didn't need it, he didn't want it – he needed only her, only that woman, that warm, sleeping mound of goodness.

The tea came in with a shy girl, whom Blossom, now fully awake, insisted on chatting to like an old friend – but as she did so, she laid her gold-ringed hand carefully on top of the sheet and toyed with the hem to show it to best effect. She breathed in the girl's envy and admiration with pleasure.

The tea swallowed, she was out of bed and nipping naked across the room to the cupboard.

'I can see by the speed with which you're dressing that it's breakfast you're after and not me,' he said with a sigh.

'Oh I've had enough of you for a bit,' she said, frowning as she did up the little buttons at the back of her frock, and ramming her feet into her espadrilles. She leaned out of the window while she waited for him to shave. 'What a lovely hot day it's going to be,' she sighed, 'just right for the seaside.'

'I have my doubts,' he said, his face smothered in lather, 'it's only June and this is England. We'll take coats.'

She came and stood beside him as he splashed the cologne on his cheeks. She held up the bottle and read the label: A GENTLEMAN'S COLOGNE. 'Oh, you're a gentleman, are you?' she quipped. 'You'd never know it between the sheets!'

'Shall we return to bed so I can try to do better?' he said, kissing her nose.

'Not before breakfast, we won't. Now buck up or I'll go down without you.' She looked at the mangled sheets. 'Shall I tidy the bed up a bit, Harold? I've never seen such a mess.'

'Don't be ridiculous. Give the maids something to gossip about. Come on, I'm ready.'

When they were sitting at the table close to the window, Blossom said that people were looking at them, and she began to fret about what the other guests would think of them being the last down to breakfast.

'It's what's expected of newly-weds,' he said with a grin and she tossed off her flurry of nerves as quickly as it had come. He showed her the menu to cheer her up completely and read her the snippet of 'A Smuggler's Song' on the inside page. She began, like a schoolgirl, to chant it portentously, but gave that up the minute the waiter arrived.

'I'll have egg, bacon, sausage and tomato – and tea – thank you,' she said with a gracious smile that landed on the waiter's ear and made it glow.

'Just a boiled egg for me please, three minutes. Yes, and tea,' Harold said crisply, wanting the waiter to take his eyes off Blossom.

'Trying to stay young and beautiful?' she sang mockingly, as if he was one of the girls.

'Got to give you a little competition now and then.' He

kissed her possessively and glared at the waiter who was looking back at her.

He moved his chair closer to hers, trying to inch nearer to that luscious body fragrance of hers that pushed itself through her creams, her shampoo, even her clothes. He slipped his hand under the tablecloth and ran it up her inner thigh; she pretended not to notice, her neck in the V-shaped neckline looking very naked, a platinum colour.

She ate as usual with the greed and gusto of a schoolgirl and had no interest in talking. He drank his tea and looked about him. He'd grown so used to observing people in his solitary eating excursions that he found his eyes roaming the room. But this time there was a perfect contentment in his watching: a raddled actress with a child in a pink dress, an American couple who drank milk and didn't shout when they spoke. He found himself listening carefully to the conversation of a contented old couple; he envied their well-established intimacies and rituals, their repetition of days. He longed suddenly for the peace of growing old with one person, the security of one face on the pillow, the tranquillity of permanent loving.

He turned to Blossom, 'We will marry, really, I mean, won't we?'

A little quiver parted her lips and her brow puckered as if to say, Are you being serious?

'I will of course kneel to you at a more appropriate time,' he said lightly, but she noticed that his lightness was serious.

'We'd have to think about it,' she said sensibly.

'But perhaps you don't believe in marriage?' he said, to tease her.

'Oh I do,' she said, with a smile full of candour, 'if it can be like my mum and dad's.' She thought a little. 'Were your parents happy? Are they, I mean?' It was strange, she could never quite place them in the past or the present.

'Oh yes,' he said, taking another triangle of toast, and remembering an atmosphere between them so concrete that he'd felt he could bruise himself against it.

'For me, marriage is for ever,' he said, 'I don't believe in divorce.'

'You a Catholic?' she said, pouring the tea and burning her fingers on the stainless steel handle.

'I'm a retired Catholic,' he said quietly.

'Oh you'll go back to it,' she laughed, 'they always do, don't they? I mean, God's really got the Catholics by the short and curlies – we had a lot of them living round us once.'

'Go back to it when I'm dying, you mean? Try to sidle into heaven?'

'Yeh, well you lot believe in hell, don't you?'

'You don't?'

'Course not, but I believe in heaven.'

'Well, that's where you'll go then.'

'Only if you'll come with me.'

'Of course I'll come with you. I couldn't stay down here without you.'

'That's settled then. Ask him for some toast, Harold, and more butter and honey.' She suddenly grabbed his arm like a child and said, 'Harold, will you love me always? The way you do now? Always?'

'Yes. Always.' He picked up her hand and turned it over, planting a kiss on the pink underside.

'Then kiss me, kiss me quickly, Harold,' she said. She shivered, quickly and violently, and then went pale. 'Kiss me, Harold, someone just walked over my grave.'

Thirty-two

Always: it was the right word – it was the only word to hold off the world's uncertainties. When I chose her, from that first day, it was not for those Mediterranean-blue eyes, that hair of a Botticelli angel – I chose her for always. Till the day I died. Till death us do part. I intended to be with her in heaven. And I wanted to give her heaven on earth.

I'm not a fool. I knew that the years would run away with her beauty faster than a dark woman's, that the sun I would buy her on long Rivieran holidays would fade her, my passion drain her. I chose her to love and adore through all the years – the sorrows, the babies, the weariness and boredoms, the stretchmarks, the lines around her eyes, the collapse of her cherry mouth. I would love her as I loved her at the beginning.

Blossom, strange thoughts come to me. I find myself wanting to be forgiven. But for what? I am quite innocent, I know that. But I also know that it's the hardest thing for people to believe in innocence. And the easiest thing for people to judge – the weaker, the smaller the mind, the harsher the judgement. It will be easier to call me names, to see me as abnormal. A freak. A monster. These words frighten people. I have looked at these words carefully and considered them; they are frightening because they are just the other side of ourselves.

I am an ordinary man; only my love was extraordinary, and what I did anyone could have done. I am not set apart from other men.

I did what I did in all innocence – I know this because it was her innocence and purity that perfected mine. Had I murdered her, that would be easier to deal with, far more understandable, a crime of passion. My passion was not a crime, but far worse. That is why I sit here and wait, delaying the moment.

Thirty-three

Walking out of the hotel after breakfast, Blossom breathed in deeply and with pleasure, 'Oh, it smells of the sea, of salt, of fish and chips.'

'It smells of mermaids,' he said.

'What do mermaids smell of?'

'Seaweed and blossom.'

'Oh look,' she said, stopping, 'it's so pretty!' Her delight was so sharp and fresh; everything was wonderful to her. The cobbled alleyways with their picture-postcard cottages, the clumps of rosemary she pulled at, crumpling the spikes between her fingers; the brief glimpses of chintz and dark furniture behind small windows draped in honeysuckle and ivy. He was perfectly at peace. He had slept all night without waking, without even seeming to dream. The sound of the wood-pigeons reminded him of the early mornings of his childhood when his mother and he had crept out to pick strawberries for breakfast.

In the car she put on the radio, which was playing 'River Deep, Mountain High' and she sang all the words in a clear low voice. And he was not dismayed – quite the contrary – and didn't for one minute miss the safe sounds of Radio 4. As he drove she told him of incidents in her childhood – a trip to Worthing, staying in a boarding house, sleeping in an attic room without Rosina, the first beautiful dress she remembered: bright green with a little white Peter Pan collar, her dad and her running races on the sand and how he always let her win.

Was she wise enough to know that confidences inspired confidences? She told him her griefs and terrors too: the dog with blood coming from its mouth on the road, the old man she had watched having a heart-attack in next door's garden; the time she had fought with Rosina and pushed her down the stairs, breaking her arm. He encouraged her to tell him more. She was quite happy to: she remembered the treats, the fairs, with such vividness because they had been infrequent and their pleasure had had to be returned to many times as she and her sister lay in bed at night chatting. Then she stopped. She wanted him to tell her stories like hers, she wanted him to have the same memories, to have done the same things. But he said nothing.

He had grown absorbed and a little melancholy as he drove down half-remembered roads across the marshes; she didn't question him but put her hand on his thigh and touched his knee with little pats now and then. Then he began the high climb up the hill to Winchelsea and she looked down at the land swathed in a pale green mist. The village of Winchelsea was quiet, it seemed uninhabited, the few small shops empty. There was something a little eerie about the place, always had been, he now remembered. It was like one of those perfect toy villages.

'This is where I used to live,' he said quietly, turning left towards the church.

'It's nice,' she said, smiling at a row of immaculate white cottages with sparkling windows and tubs full of geraniums, petunias and lobelia.

'Does anyone live here? It's so quiet.' She had even begun to whisper.

He laughed shortly. 'Yes, they do. It was always like this,' he added vaguely, 'the houses hardly ever changed hands and if there were children they didn't play on the streets.'

'It's not even a Sunday,' she said, feeling unsettled by the pretty village, with its dogless streets and closed doors.

'And your dad was the doctor here?' she asked.

'Yes, one of them. Winchelsea's not as small as it looks. My father shared a practice in Rye, went in on Wednesdays and Fridays, I think, and there was a surgery at our house too.'

Harold had stopped the car and pulled up to look at the church. He'd always found the ruins quite beautiful and grand and wondered now how it might feel to think you had designed a building that had stood since the thirteenth century, been nearly destroyed by the French and yet retained its nobility and power.

'It seems too big for this little place,' she said with the simple logic he loved.

'It was a much more important place when the church was built, a great port, but there's a sort of relentless decay in its history, and there's something sad about it.'

He realized that he was just delaying the moment when he would have to look at the house where he had lived, and, with one of the sudden movements that always startled Blossom, he'd yanked off the handbrake and started the car. He drove slowly round the corner and the back of the church to the house on the corner. His house.

He stopped again, with a jerk, and said quickly, 'This is the one.' It was a gracious old house. The twisted trunk of a dead tree seemed to have become fossilized into the grey stone of one wall. Greedy ivy rambled up the front walls and nibbled at the window panes. The front garden was small, with standard-roses neatly laid out, and a path that led to other gardens out of sight, behind high walls.

'I can't see properly,' she said, 'can we get out?'

Her voice had startled him. 'Of course.' For a moment he had forgotten her, forgotten even himself as he now was.

'It won't make you sad?' She was gently solicitous. 'Once we went back to a house we'd lived in when I was tiny and it made me sad. My mum said, "Well, they must love it, look at all that they've done to it." But I really *hated* them for changing all our things. I couldn't understand her.'

He smiled tenderly, 'I know what you mean, but no, I'll be fine. As long as you're here.' It was wonderful for her to suddenly feel his need in this way, this simple, maternal way which she trusted herself with. She got out of the car and when he came up to her she caught up his hand in hers.

A wind blew, shaking some high trees in the garden opposite. He suddenly remembered the first day they had come to this house – his mother and father and him. His mother had been so excited – on days like that she seemed to skip, to be airborne on a strange high happiness. His father had picked her up and carried her through the doorway, an alarming fierce happiness in his face. How old had Harold been? Just above her knee. She had thrown down her bare arm like a pale rope to the small boy and said: 'Oh, we mustn't leave out James. James, come here, my darling. I shall carry you in too.' He wanted to tell Blossom this, but the memory was not simple, it was mixed with ambiguous and vaguely frightening echoes; he was happy to let it go.

The garden was fortified by high holly fences and stone walls, the flower garden separated from the long vegetable garden by yet another lichened wall.

'What a lovely long garden,' she said with no trace of envy, 'my dad would love to get his hands on all those veggies. Look at them all – cabbages and leeks and lettuces.'

And now it was easy, she'd said the right thing and he could reciprocate; his voice seemed to bang in its eagerness to speak to her, 'My mother loved to grow vegetables. I remember once in the winter wanting to bring her in some carrots and turnips but they were all black and eaten away so I buried them instead.' He laughed, 'She grew wonderful raspberries, lines and lines of them and little scarlets.'

'Where is she now? Where are they now?' she asked, trailing her hand along the wall as they walked on the grass verge beside it.

'They're in, well, in Malta.' It was as if he'd just thought of it.

'In Malta! So I couldn't possibly have met them then.' She felt slightly deceived.

He looked at her sideways, 'Did you think we were coming here to see them?'

'Well, no,' she frowned, 'no, not really, because you hadn't said or anything, but when you said you'd lived round here when you were little I thought they'd still be here.' Sometimes it was very difficult to ask him things directly, sometimes you had to circle around what you really wanted to know to find it out.

'But I told you they didn't live here any more, didn't I?' He spoke in an indifferent way, looking up at the magnificent yew tree which dominated the garden. Once he'd been frightened of it, but later he'd built a house beneath it. A perfect house, his mother had said, he should be an architect one day.

'They went to Malta ages ago,' he said, as they walked down the lane at the bottom of the garden. 'I went to school in Rye when I was eight, by eleven I was in boarding school and they'd gone abroad. My father's retired now of course. He dabbles at things, loves collecting – butterflies, stamps, old and beautiful things.'

She was walking in her quick way, pulling at the leaves, taking her arm out of his to do so and then replacing it.

'The school in Rye, was it nice? And the boarding school?' The idea made her shudder.

'I was quite happy at school,' he said in a formal way, as if answering a question on a form. But then he had an agonizing moment: he remembered being surrounded by a gang of older boys who'd pressed him in against the wall, their upper lips darkened by the beginnings of moustache hair, their skin greasy. With their mouths close to his face they'd hissed, 'Your mother's in the loony bin, in the bin, bin, bin. Your mother's a loony.' He closed his eyes with the pain of it: their grey-flannel legs pressing in on him, their knees grinding into his thighs, their faces grinning over him like the faces in nightmares.

Miraculously, as if a blanket had been flapped back from over his face, he was able to conjure up the clear side of a strangely split memory: his father saying, 'Come round the desk, Harold, sit on my knee, boy. The teacher has told me there was a nasty incident at school today.' Harold went sullen and lowered his jaw, about to deny its occurrence once and for all, but his father went on, 'I don't want this to upset you, it was a foolish and ignorant cruelty on the part of those boys.' And then his voice had grown tender, womanly even, as he'd whispered, 'Only you and I know, my boy, only we two, only you and I know your mother, we who love her. She can't be hurt by them, nor can we. She is ours. We can keep her always. She is still with us and will never leave us.'

The Harold of now winced to remember his small self sobbing against the rough tweed of his father's coat, feeling the pleasure of its hurt on his hot smarting face. It was one of the very few times that his father had been able to overcome his fear of emotional displays.

'Shall we look inside the church, Blossom?' They had walked up the gravel path, past the toppled tombstones, the broken skeleton of the transept, and were about to enter the church itself. She walked ahead of him and he hovered behind her, admiring the beauty of the stonework, touching it reverently. A feeling of space and air flooded him as he walked into the church and a wonderful molten glow from the stained-glass windows warmed the great Gothic arches and dark pews.

He was surprised to see that she knelt in one of the pews, lowering her head in prayer. He sat down next to her with his hands between his knees, and waited. A woman in a blue smock was arranging tall vases of iris and carnations. Apart from her, it was empty. He had never attended this church with his father after his conversion. They'd gone to Mass. But often in the afternoon he had wandered around the outer rim of the church, studying the tombs in the north aisle, watching the cold stone face of the warrior who lay with his legs crossed. It had seemed so forlorn, as indeed it still felt now.

Blossom lifted her head, got up and sat down next to him.

'Did you pray for me?' he whispered.

'Of course.'

He smiled, 'Do you say your prayers at night, my darling? I bet you do.'

'Oh yes,' she said, looking around her, her eyes drawn back to the brilliant blue glass in the centre window.

'What do you say?' He moved closer and took her hand.

She snuggled closer to him, feeling it wasn't quite right to chat in church, 'Oh, it's silly really, just a child's prayer.' She pulled her skirt down, he was looking at her knees.

'Go on, tell me,' he threaded his fingers through hers companionably.

'Well, I used to kneel up in bed when I was little, and, because of being scared of the dark, I'd whisper, "If I should die before I wake, I pray the Lord my soul will take." I'd say it ever so fast and then lie down quick.'

He could see her doing it; her fingers long and plump and pressed together, her soft matted curls – how extraordinary that mouth must have looked in the innocent setting of a small girl's face.

'But now when I say it,' she smiled brightly, 'I say, if *we* should die before we wake, I pray the Lord our souls will take.' With a nudge, she added, 'Someone has to pray for you, Harold.'

'Quite right.' He moved to get up, but she seemed to hesitate, to look shyly at the floor where she shuffled her feet about.

'What is it? Do you want to stay?' He sat again and looked at her in that patient and considerate way he had.

She pulled at his arm and fingered the cotton shirt; then looked over to where the woman in the smock had been arranging the flowers, but had now disappeared.

'Harold,' she hesitated, 'will you put the ring on again, in here? I'd like that.'

Harold (and how she loved him for this decisiveness) didn't hesitate for a moment. He took the gold band with its circle of pearls off her finger, kissed the palm of her hand, then put it on again slowly, saying, 'I take thee as my Blossom, my bride, to love and to treasure as long as we both shall live.' He had looked at her quite steadfastly as he spoke, his eyes never wavering.

Hers were very wide and startled. She tried to speak but her voice fluttered so much that she had to start again. 'I take thee, Harold, to be my husband, in sickness and in health, for as long as we both shall live.'

'Now you are mine,' he said with gentle satisfaction, 'now you are mine.'

'Yes,' she whispered, dazed, a strange fulfilled smile on her lips. Her mouth trembled so much that he kissed it, tenderly, and then with violence, feeling her fingers bite into the bones at the back of his neck, feeling her teeth sink into his lips.

Then they walked up the long aisle hand in hand, and out into the brilliant sunshine, past the gravestones and green grass, and out on to the pavement, which was still quite deserted.

Thirty-four

She told me, later, why she had wanted that ceremony in the church.

'It was just,' she said, with an odd melancholy in her eyes, 'that I suddenly knew that we wouldn't, you know, be married properly – that something would stop us and it wouldn't happen. And I wanted to *so* at that moment, it was perfectly right, at that moment, and it might never have been right like that again. We might never have felt like that again – oh, Harold, things change, people change – and then you wish and wish and it's all too late.'

Her face was turned away from me and her profile was as I'd seen it the very first time and the same feeling of indescribable joy and hope filled me again.

'But what could stop us?' I asked her, feeling such peace with her, lying beside her on the Elizabethan bed, arm in arm, our fingers entwined.

'I don't know. I just thought that we wouldn't marry like ordinary people do. I don't know why. Sometimes I feel things.' She said she had had a strange premonition that she, or I, would enter that church again, one of us, alone, and that the small ceremony would retain all its power to bind and haunt us. But she was sad and withdrawn from me. Our moods had not connected, and though I worshipped her and worshipped her with my body, I could not comfort or keep her. And her eyes in the darkness grew sombre as leaves under moonlight.

She was afraid without knowing why. And later, when I feigned sleep, I could feel her thoughts hurting her; later still, I heard her quietly crying. But was too afraid to ask her why.

Blossom, if I entered that church again I would die. If I sat where we sat and loved one another so intensely, where we symbolically became one, your God would strike me dead. Kill me but not take my soul. And your soul, my darling, where is it now? Don't worry, I know, it's mine, you gave it to me. By then we were so entangled we neither knew which was you and which was me. Oh Blossom, for one touch, one sense of you now. I almost wish that your God, your kind sweet God, *would* strike me dead.

Thirty-five

The sea. He watched as she clambered up the grassy slope like a puppy, her shoes leaving thick lozenges of mud where she had danced and leapt on higher. At the top, when she could see the sea, she turned and waved at him. The wind whooshed her scarlet dress up over her head; it sucked at her cheeks with the tenacity of a wet sheet. The white lace of her knickers blinded him, winded him; his heart was so huge it pummelled against his ribs to get at her. At last she held down her whirling dress, waved again, and raced off after the wind like a hound after a hat.

He couldn't be bothered to lock the car; he pursued her up the grassy bank, the wind licking his hair flat and away from his forehead so that his face looked very young and invigorated; the dull gold of his eyes began to shine and reflect something of their real depths. He looked up and he couldn't see her at all; she'd disappeared over the crown to the shingle below.

At the top he stopped and looked down. He saw a dab of scarlet far out, beyond the shingle, out where the sand lay golden, waiting for the sea. The tide was coming in and Blossom was rushing out to meet it – a little girl in an elasticated swimsuit, a bucket in her hand and her hair tied up in a ponytail. The waves came rushing up to hug her feet, to lick and love her; they rolled over on their backs and turned inside out for her. One sneaked up and caught her coldly by the ankle; she gasped, the air rushing out of her flushed cheeks as she flirted with it, running backwards away from the foam.

He groaned: how far to reach her! This distance that she set between them – did she need it so much then? Did he confine her? Trap that free spirit in his own needs? Let her go – let her go, he whispered to himself. Let her stay there, alone and happy, on the brink of new discoveries.

But he couldn't. He hurled himself down the dusty avalanche of shingle and by the time he reached the sand he was panting and sweating. He could see her more clearly now. And look – she hadn't gone from him, she turned and beckoned, then crouched down for a moment so that the long dab of scarlet telescoped into a neat square. He imagined her vanilla thighs, the round scoops of her knees. Suddenly she began to run towards him. And in that instant he regained his youth, his lost boyhood – and he pelted towards her, laughing, the wind bringing tears to his eyes.

He caught her – a sea-fresh woman brimming over with happiness, her hair tickling his cheeks; the beautiful cupid's bows of her mouth red and sharp, hot and wet inside as he tumbled her to the damp sand. The wind flung her dress up above her waist, the sun snatched up the white lace and reflected it into his eyes, the sand was not softer or more yielding than her body beneath his.

'My God, me bum's all wet and crunchy!' she moaned. Her face was pink all over, rubbed raw by kisses, her curls tight and damp.

At the very top of his voice he yelled: 'She is the most delicious woman in the world.' He shouted it again, at the sea, the sky, the wind, and his words whirled away.

'And he's the most greedy man,' she yelled, just as loudly, to the long empty beach.

'What will become of us?' he asked quietly, feeling his throat throb.

'Everything,' she said, laughing, 'everything.' She tugged at him, 'Come on, I'll race you to the top.'

'Oh, I couldn't, Blossom, I'd pass out.'

'You need more fresh air, that's your trouble,' she said, pulling at the skirt of her dress, shaking the last of the sand out of her knickers and pushing her hair back impatiently as it flew into her mouth and eyes. 'Oh all right, Harold, we must remember your age,' she said, straightening his hair, brushing the sand off his shirt. 'I'll take your arm, shall I, and we'll stroll back up.'

'We could be an elderly couple out for a constitutional,' he said affectionately.

'I thought that was something to do with politics,' she said with mock innocence.

'You like to tease me, don't you?'

'Yeh, you're too bleeding serious. When I first spoke to you, in Marks, I wanted to hug you, you seemed a man in need of lots of good hugs.'

'Did I?' He could hardly believe it of himself.

She shivered, 'Oh, I always get cold after you've had me.' She clutched at his arm.

'Oh, that's what happens, is it? I have *you*?' He grinned and tucked her hair behind her ear.

'Course it is.'

At the top she turned and looked back; and cried out, 'Oh look, Harold, how fast the sea's coming in, it's nearly got to our place. Soon all our marks will be washed away, all gone.'

'Oh no,' he said with finality, 'when it gets there, it'll stop.'

Thirty-six

They were walking down a High Street crowded with Saturday shoppers. Blossom, hanging on to Harold's arm, kept stopping to look into windows, with a face radiant yet somehow trance-like. Then she pulled him into the upward sweep of a cobbled street and kissed him.

'Oh Harold, this day's been so lovely, I don't want it ever to end.' It was as if she saw no one but him, felt nothing but his touch on her arm, as if, in all that hurrying crowd, only the two of them existed.

'There'll be other days just as wonderful,' he said, wondering where his new gift for happiness sprang from, if not from her.

On the next corner he stopped and told her, 'See that chemist, they still call it an apothecary – I can remember going into that shop when I was about twelve or thirteen. My father used to have long conversations with the chemist. It was in there that he said to me that he was glad I had no interest in being a doctor. When I asked him why, he said – and it was a most curious thing for him to say – that being a doctor took all the wonder and mystery out of a woman's body. That word: body. It sounded so acutely personal coming from him that I was embarrassed.' He looked awkward then as if he'd forgotten himself, 'I don't know,' he shrugged with a smile, 'perhaps he was just trying to have a facts-of-life conversation with me.'

'Oh,' she said with a wicked grin, 'so you still don't know then?'

They had moved into the side streets which were steep but less crowded. She kept stopping to look at antique furniture, Chinese vases and paintings – and asked him about them as if he were an expert, as he quickly proved to be.

'But I'd never have a shop,' he said. 'I couldn't bear the idea of someone buying anything I'd chosen and loved. I wouldn't even let them in the shop!'

She was getting tired and he was very quick to pick up indications in her. 'Shall I take you for lunch somewhere?' he said, taking his eyes with difficulty off an exquisite hand-blown glass vase in a shop window. He had spotted the beauty among the indifferent collection instantly.

'Oh no,' she said with an eager low laugh, 'let's not go to lunch, Harold, let's just go into all these nooky shops and buy quiche and pies and cakes and cheese, grapes and peaches and lots of wine and French bread, and then go back to our lovely room and have a great big feast and spend the whole afternoon in bed. We can't waste such a beautiful bed. Quick, Harold, let's get away from all these daft people. Let's go home to our hotel.'

Thirty-seven

Home. Wherever she was she made a nest and I fell into it.
Even my own house, my home, was not a home once she'd
gone. She had a way of placing things – flowers, my books,
or even draping her clothes, which made a warmth and intimacy about us.

That day in Rye was the most perfect and peaceful of my
life. Glutted on peaches, brie, warm bread and dark wine; her
body, her gentle generous capacity for pleasure, her almost
wounding ripeness – like that moment when a bud is swollen
almost to splitting before it releases its secret. She was all this
and more. Her tenderness made a man of me; slowly I found
myself telling her things I had barely discussed with myself,
and she made me feel in a short while there would be nothing
so frightening that she couldn't know and understand it.

I began to marvel at my sad attempts with one or other
of those complicated women of my past – how carefully I must
have chosen them to keep me safe, and dry, and alone. Blossom, glowing with warm laziness, her head in my lap as we
lay on the fat springy bed, peeling grapes for me which she ate
herself: how could I have lived so long in ignorance of such
tranquillity? She made me laugh, she made me weep – she
made me real. She bent and nipped the end of my cock and
said, 'Oh, I'm so sorry, I thought it was a grape!' It was as if
intimacy and deep pleasure were so new to her that she must
surround them with laughter and brightness – it was her way
of keeping us both connected a little to the world.

Did she know, as I did, that we two were dangerously
divided from the world? Gone utterly from it into our own
deep quiet place? Even the past lost its power. During those
days every step I took back into the past led me away from

it. She led me out of the maze, yet often I never even told her what I was feeling. I didn't need to. It may even be that she had nothing to do with that change in me, it might have been my own change. Enough to know that before her I had never retravelled that road at all – but during those two days and nights with her I constantly remembered and relived all that had made me what I now was. And, as I revisited it, I knew that it was over for ever. When we left, I left it all behind me. Loving Blossom had cured me of my past. But if the past lost its pull, somehow the future was unimaginable in those days too, unimaginable and quite immaterial. The moment was purely perfect. We were captured within our own spell and I came to realize that it was a prison – that once outside, the world would intrude and divide us. I felt that to leave Rye would break me. That such perfection and power as we had known there could only be sealed by death. And it was this that set me apart, from her, from the world. This was my fatal flaw: I could not dare to believe in change.

Thirty-eight

I spent that night watching her sleep. She had drunk a lot, and anyway she always slept deeply, waking up in the morning quickly and easily, as I imagine a child would wake. The moon was watching her as jealously as I. By dawn I wanted to sleep, but couldn't – not that I was tired, contact with her only made me more quick, more alive. I took the covers gently off her naked limbs and looked at her in the soft early morning light. The colour of her skin was changing with the changing light.

Her hand with my ring on it was flung out with the palm open; the buds of her breasts were very small and pale. The soundness of her sleep and those generous outflung arms tempted me to look at her more intimately than she would allow me to. I longed to part her smallest lips and see her rosy centre. I wanted to know all about her body, its tiniest crevices, the different tones and textures of her skin, where it yielded and where it stayed firm – the entire mystery of her being, all that was hidden and secret from me.

Once, when I had tried to look at her in this way, she had stiffened against me. It was too intimate, it frightened her. It reminded me of the time she had confessed to me that once the things that we now did so easily had seemed freaky to her. I should have waited, she would have come to it, but I so longed and ached to know all of her that I couldn't wait. It was a great insensitivity.

For she woke with a start and a sharp cry. I had parted her little lips – more gently it couldn't have been done – but some subconscious alarm pulled her back from sleep and she looked at me furiously. As if I had trespassed on her, as if I had broken a trust. The look so alarmed me that I quickly covered her. She turned and was instantly asleep.

I never knew whether she remembered it, or thought it a dream, for she never referred to it. But at that moment I knew that I had gone too far, that I had the potential to destroy all I held most precious because of my obsession to possess her, to possess her so utterly that nothing would be left of herself for herself. Could time have cured me of this malady? I can't tell, even though I felt she could cure me of anything. But I don't know, because somehow I've always felt that part of me was incurable. Even today, knowing what I know, having done what I have done, I would still be the same. That is and was my tragedy. But soon, all too soon, it became hers.

Thirty-nine

She was sitting up in bed, resting her head on the curve of Harold's shoulder.

'What a life,' she sighed, 'breakfast in bed and the papers brought up. I could get used to this.'

'Hm,' he said, still reading the front page of the *Sunday Times*; it was impossible to get any further because she kept talking to him.

'I suppose we'll have to get up,' she said, wrapping an arm around his chest and tunnelling further down under the covers.

'I'll hate leaving this room, this lovely big bed – look how beautifully the wood is carved, with thistles and roses, and you feel so safe in a room with so much wood.' She looked at the full-blown roses in the stone fireplace, the sun taking over more and more of the carpet. Beauty made her sad sometimes and she went quiet, listening to Harold's breathing.

'I'll have a bath,' she said a bit later, 'then you can dry me till I squeak.'

Suddenly he was alert, his arm pinning her down, 'Don't go just yet.'

'But all the sunshine's being wasted.'

'You have a mania for scrimping and saving when it comes to this bed or the sunshine. I hope you're not going to turn into one of those penny-pinching wives.' He turned the page over with difficulty.

'How could I, Harold, when you're so rich?'

'Am I?' He was quite startled.

'Well, to me you are. You can have what you want.'

'That makes me rich?' he laughed.

'It makes you darn comfortable,' she said with a tart edge to her voice.

'I'm only comfortable when I'm with you.' He discarded the newspaper. 'Don't get up yet, we have to leave here soon enough.'

'Oh,' she groaned, piling all her curls on top of her head with her hands, 'I really don't want to go.'

'Well, let's stay then.'

She looked at him with curiosity, 'You mean it? You would stay? And not go to work tomorrow, even with that witchy Alexander woman hounding you to give her an estimate?'

'Of course I mean it,' he said coolly, lying back on the pillows. 'What's the point of having your own business if you can't do what you want to.' Oh yes, he could play truant now, he could tell Mrs Alexander to go and stuff herself, he could tell Max to get on with it and not tell any of his bloody stupid lies – he could, and would, do anything and everything for Blossom. This was, he thought, the essence of a free man, to follow his own inclinations, to make his own decisions, to follow his heart and see where it led him.

Blossom said, 'Oh, but we couldn't!' She giggled with pleasure at the idea of Mrs O'Brien, her Supervisor, getting all red and flustered as she always did when someone she trusted was disloyal enough to get ill.

'Oh but we could,' he said, watching her face with interest.

'Tell a lie, you mean, say I'm sick or something?'

'Anything – or nothing. Just not go back.'

'Oh, I couldn't do nothing. I'd have to tell Bev or she'd be ever so worried. And anyway, if you don't turn up for work and don't ring or anything, they'll check up to make sure you're all right, you know.'

'My word, what a sense of responsibility that shop has.'

'I think it's nice,' she frowned at him.

'Of course it is,' he kissed her on the nose; he didn't care for frowns.

'No,' she decided, 'we must go back. I've a sense of responsibility too, you know.'

'I know you have.' But he was disappointed, though she

didn't notice. Then he brightened and moved so she could curl up against him, 'We can go away a little later. I'll take you to France or Italy. How about that? I could take you to Tuscany, we'll walk in the olive groves at Lucca, where they have the most delicious olive oil in the world, or I could get you fat on pasta and cakes and ice-cream.'

She thought a little, 'Yes, let's do that, Harold, I've got all my holiday to come and I've got some money saved. Let's do that.'

He closed his eyes with pleasure – Blossom honey-coloured, brown Blossom, ochre Blossom, Blossom with shiny taut skin running to the sea, Blossom naked or wearing her dazzling colours against white walls and bougainvillaea terraces – Blossom in that sharp white light, drugged with the heat and the sun – a completely new and exciting Blossom to discover.

But she was wriggling to escape, 'I'm getting up now,' she announced with determination.

'Not yet, you aren't.'

The suitcases were in the boot of the car. Blossom stood quietly looking up at the hotel, sad to be leaving. She was wearing a white and green candy-striped blouse with a wing collar, emerald cravat, and bermuda shorts in a dark fuchsia shade. She climbed into the car and pushed out her bare legs in front of her.

'Where are we off to now, then?'

'I want to go back to a place we went to yesterday,' he said quietly.

'O.K.,' she said, and put on the radio; she began to hum with it.

Harold drove carefully down narrow lanes with soft green slopes either side; the sheep were all grazing in the sunshine and the willows leaning over the canal were tinged with gold, the green as vivid as the stripes of her blouse. When he reached the place they had walked to the day before, he stopped the car, and said, 'Can we just go down to the canal again? There's something I must do there.'

Her face became grave with comprehension, she knew exactly what was in his mind, 'You want to go back to where we saw that strange skeleton in the water, don't you?'

He loved her so for knowing, 'Yes, I do, it's haunted me ever since. I can't stop thinking about it. I even dreamt about it last night.'

'So did I,' she said, looking away from him. 'I dreamt that it was sinking deeper and deeper into the mud, only – oh, it was horrible, only it wasn't a skeleton, it wasn't dead, it was alive, and it was crying.' The horror of the dream returned and she shuddered. 'Perhaps, Harold,' she said cautiously, 'perhaps we were both dreaming about it at the same time. What did you dream?'

'In my dream it wouldn't sink either, it kept coming up to the air, again and again, but in my dream it was a corpse, all white and small. It was dead, but it wouldn't sink.' He took her hand firmly, 'Come on, if I don't bury it, I'll never get it out of my head.' But at the fence he hesitated, he turned to her and said, 'It frightens me, it had a rib-cage just like yours.'

'Like mine?'

'Yes, its little ribs were like yours.'

She shivered, 'But what *was* it, Harold? I mean, it didn't look like an animal, and it was too small to be human – that odd little skull, like a human skull – oh, I don't know.' They were walking along the grass and across to the trees that lined the canal. He took her hand as they walked down the slope to the water.

Blossom was still struggling with the different images of her dream, and she said, 'It was far too small for a human baby.' They had reached the small canal and she looked confused and said, 'Was it here?'

'No, a little further along.' They walked in silence.

Harold stopped, 'Look – there!'

It was not as startling as when they had first seen it. The water had moved it a little and it lay at a different angle, partly hidden by tangled green scum. Beneath the water, not very far down as the water was only a foot or so deep, lay the tiny white skeleton. They stood hand in hand and stared down at it; it had been facing upwards but now it was slightly on its side. There was something stark and forlorn about it and for a moment he was tempted to leave it where it was, to let the water take it to herself.

But it was Blossom who said fearfully, 'We must bury it, Harold, we must, we can't leave it in there, poor little thing.' It was as if, because of what he'd said about its rib-cage being like hers, it had become part of her. Harold crouched down and began to roll the sleeves of his shirt up and reached down into the water, which immediately muddied over.

'I don't think I'll be able to reach it,' he said.

She backed away. 'I'm scared of it,' she said, and when he looked at her he saw that all the colour had gone from her face.

He stood up and put his arm round her for a moment, then took off his shirt, lay down flat on the ground and sunk his arm right up to the shoulder in the cold water. His other arm came down and very carefully he scooped up the soft mud beneath the white-boned creature and brought it up. Blossom stood a long way back, her hands to her mouth – like a primitive person afraid of the retributions of sacrilege and plunder.

Harold flung the water off his arms once he had set it down on the ground; now it looked more frail and more human, but just as inexplicable because of its minute frame. Blossom was ignoring it, she was concentrating on Harold's real live body: the hard smoothness of his shoulders, the soft down on his chest, the way his long, tapered arms were balanced on the earth. She wouldn't come closer.

'Put your shirt on, Harold,' she called, 'you'll get cold.'

He put on his shirt and began to look around him for a sharp stone. When he'd found one, he took Blossom by the hand and led her away from the water to find a suitable burial place. She chose a flat place under a tree and watched as he scraped away at the earth to make a hole. While he did so, she was recovered enough to go and look for some flowers, yellow primroses and a few buttercups.

He had buried the skeleton – it was no bigger than his hand – and was now flattening the earth on top. She had kept a superstitious distance while he did this, but now came forward and carefully arranged her leaves and flowers on top of the small mound. She was now more frightened, but it was Harold's intensity that alarmed her; she couldn't fathom who or what he was trying to bury in the ground in that obsessive, compelled way. Yesterday, she'd had no idea that it had had such importance to him, and yet the small skeleton had haunted both their dreams. She began to feel curiously close to him because of it, as if she was inextricably bound up in this burial ritual, as if it was as meaningful as their marriage ceremony in Winchelsea. It tied them more closely together: they had performed the rituals of marriage and of burial together and the two seemed strangely connected.

He stood. She took his hand and they both looked down at the small grave. Something, he felt, had come to a culmination, something unfinished was buried and gone. He felt whole with relief, his life sparkled with hope, with a peace that he could only recall from a dim warm past when his mother's touch had woken him in the morning.

He sat down on the ground and pulled Blossom down beside him. He knew he would really have to try for the first time in his life to help another human being understand him. It was so hard, he was so self-contained, so shut within himself, but he felt strong enough now to try. It was as if his loneliness was suddenly very tangible to him: his solitary childhood and difficult adolescence; his state of shock when his mother disappeared.

'When I lived here,' he began quietly, 'I was very unhappy. I've only realized how unhappy in the last few days – by being so happy with you. This place always seemed haunted to me, I never came back to it. My mother you see, she was very, well, very ill here, and my father sort of went peculiar here too. Or

I thought so, I was bewildered and very frightened by him: he became a Catholic and made me become one too – when I was very small. Suddenly we started going to instruction every day and then Mass. I don't know what happened really, but a kind of confusion happened in me. The Church and my mother's disappearance somehow seemed linked – and then, later, there was something about taking communion that seemed to return her to me. I felt that eating those little dry wafers kept her inside me, part of me. I was very very sad then and a little mad too I'm sure. Children can be mad, you know, it's not just an adult complaint.' He smiled his wry secret smile.

Blossom said nothing, just twisted a strand of grass between her fingers. She felt so sorry for him, she could tell how brave he was being to tell her these things; she wanted so to wrap him in her arms, but didn't dare.

Harold leaned back. 'I began to hate my father here too, I blamed him for what had happened to my mother. Because I couldn't blame her for anything. I adored her, you see. And all these years I've believed that she couldn't have loved me because she left me. But now I know that she just couldn't help it.' He felt as though all of him was splintering under the weight of his emotion. Blossom reached across and took his hand, she kissed it softly and looked at him tenderly.

'Oh Harold, of course she loved you,' she said with a choked sob, 'of course she did. How could she *not*?'

His heart cleared: in that moment of her complete love and faith in him he felt completely healed. It was as if he'd needed someone to say that to him all his life. He let his head fall forward on to her hands and he began to cry as he had never been able to cry as a little boy.

Forty

I began life again in Rye. Two days with you did more good than all those years of suffering, more than that terrible time in the hospital when I was seventeen, when they tried to make me talk and think, and I was desperate only never to feel again. I didn't think with you, Blossom, I just felt. That time in Rye when the past came back to me, it was not thought that returned, it was feeling, and it was the feeling that cured me.

I buried the corpse of my childhood, my mother, my God – they returned to the earth in peace. And I brought you home to this house in Kensington, which has now become a different kind of mausoleum. We had bought all those flowers along the way, you made me keep stopping so you could buy flowers and more flowers and when we got home we filled all the vases with them.

Now all I can do is think and think and think. I don't feel, Blossom, I don't dare. Perhaps I have died. Perhaps that terrible night I died also. That was the last time I felt.

After I knew you had gone, I was not just a widower, but an orphan too. Blossom, I rage, I rage. I will *never* say to you, 'Go in peace.' I cannot let you rest. I will pull you back, I will never let you leave me.

Forty-one

The doorbell has rung with shocking violence. It's the kind of sound that can't be ignored any longer. I've ignored the telephone and played my Bowie very loud to cover its insistence. Lately it has begun to shriek every hour, on the hour, meticulous and terrifying. It's quite unbearable.

I am so afraid of it, I'm so afraid. Blossom, what can I do with this terrible feeling that now you've gone I've become suddenly old? It's not my own mortality that haunts me. Nor have I tried to banish you to shelter myself from grief and shock – I've assimilated you in the most complete, most loving way possible: I have become you.

But how hollow my hand because I cannot touch you, how elderly I have become without your laughter, your kiss, your mischief, your delicious youth which gave me my first taste of delinquency and joy.

Oh Blossom, come back to me just for one moment to make my fear bearable. I fear reality, I fear what lies behind that urgent ringing. I want no eyes but mine on you, I will allow no eyes, no touch on your body but mine. They will not touch you, I swear it, they will not look at you. I would die, I will die to prevent it.

The doorbell has stopped. In this little space of silence let there be peace, just peace.

Forty-two

Your phantom wore the moon's cold mask,
   My phantom wore the same;
Forgetful of the feverish task
   In hope of which they came,
Each image held the other's eyes
And watched a grey distraction rise . . .
                                    ROBERT GRAVES

Blossom, why did you change? I detest change. I thought you were the same. I've lived my life by timetables and watches, by girders and scaffolding. I was an indestructible building with deep foundations to keep me impervious to change and age. I liked to think there was a preservation order on me.

But at a single touch you reduced me to rubble; with your little finger you pushed and I fell hurtling. I'm a preserver. Did I ever show you my collection of butterflies and moths? The little sparrow that died when I was eight, and which my father had preserved and mounted for me? I still have it somewhere.

You can see all this in my work – that house you liked so much in Fulham. I was not a man to replace a gentle Victorian building with a mess of concrete and steel, nor destroy good bricks and mortar to put up cold steel and unfeeling glass. The human spirit needs harmony and grace, and it needs continuity; we all hate it when buildings are demolished, something in each of us dies to see it go so ignominiously under the blows of bulldozers. What I like best is to regenerate what is old and trusted and loved, to continue its life, its familiar shape on the skyline – by careful reconstruction, letting it continue to enhance the permanence in life. Buildings can be recycled, they should not be pulled down and buried. Change must be gradual and tolerable or the human spirit cannot bear it.

Why did you change, my darling? Did I make you? I would far rather blame me than you. So innocent, so sweet, you were. But you did change. There was a time when I knew your essential self as I knew your body. During those weekends when we lay together most of the day and listened to the birds and the two children from next door playing catch. My happiness was simple and complete then: you were mine. No one could possess you as I possessed you on those long hot afternoons. I watched you discover your body as I discovered mine for the first time, and knew for the first time that it was mine. I gave it up to you with the easiest abandon. You were like a girl reaching to throw a ball up into a net: I listened as your cries reached higher-gasping, making a strange ah, ah, ah sound as you grew more breathless. Your convulsions rocked my body as it thrusted towards your centre. I became a young athlete who could lift you towards the sky to help you fling your ball through the highest hoop.

But you grew afraid of your own abandon, and you grew afraid of what it did to me. There was a sadness in your eyes as we lay in each other's arms and looked, speechlessly, into the mirror of our naked faces. I thought gentleness would comfort you. I would kiss you over and over in my favourite place beneath your long collarbone. I would cover your body with my kisses, never missing an inch. When you slept I cut up peaches and melon for you, soaked grapes in chilled champagne and laid them out on a table beside your bed so you could wake up to their scent. Your whoop of laughter and pleasure was the only reward I needed, your outstretched arms the dearest reassurance in the world. I could hear the boy next door shrieking, 'You're out, you're out,' and all the fear in those words evaporated in your smile.

I had you then in a way I felt no man ever had a woman. But change is so insidious. I didn't want to see it so the first heralds escaped my attention, so wrapped up in you, in your service, had I become. Nothing else mattered. I couldn't live a day without your face, my hunger for you never abated, I forgot all about work. My long starvation required constant nourishment or I faded – but what I didn't see was that you too were fading, as a delicate bloom too much handled will simply fall to pieces. This was my mistake, if it can be called that: my terror of loss made loss inevitable; my possessiveness of you made you long to be free.

I suddenly saw it one day – how much had changed. I was standing by my window, waiting for her, waiting for her as I always did. Then she came around the corner. Before, I know I always watched her in a particular way, my attention undivided, focused entirely upon her as she walked in that wonderfully brisk way of hers across the cobbles. Now I saw that my attention had become fragmented, because now I watched the glances of the garage mechanics, I tried to lip-read what they whispered to one another as she passed. Then I looked desperately to see if she would look backwards at them. Once, I thought that she did.

I noticed that her walk had slowed. I saw that the autumn had come to her hair as surely as it had come to the trees, that the gold had become tawny, it was less wild and vibrant. Her face was a little anxious and as she neared my house, her top teeth would nip into the soft pink of her bottom lip. The beautiful bold blues and scarlets of her dresses had been replaced by an anonymous navy-blue, and that lovely vulgar movement she had of sliding her finger under her nose had vanished as surely as had the sprinkling of freckles on her nose.

She was my Blossom, but perhaps she was no longer so truly mine. I had frightened her and she had withdrawn. And all she had really wanted was to be a little herself, to be a little alone, not to be so consumed by me. She was beginning to suffer. I could not help her. I was too terrified of losing her. Please forgive me this, this great stupidity that comes from too great, too blind a love. Please forgive me this, Blossom.

Forty-three

Blossom hesitated on the doorstep; she had her own key but was reluctant to use it – once she wouldn't have been, she would have just flung open the door and called him loudly. Her eyes were in shadow, it was almost as if her face was in shadow too. While she hesitated, Harold opened the door from the inside. She walked in quickly and kissed him. He noticed that her cheeks were cold, and that lovely smell of her, warm and animal, was muted.

He put his arm around her and asked, 'How did it go?'

'It was terrible,' she said.

'Come and sit in the big chair and I'll make you some tea.'

She sat down and looked up at the Buddha, her eyes full of sadness. Her face was very pale and her bottom lip looked rather bruised because she bit it so frequently.

He poured her her tea in a delicate Royal Doulton cup; he thought it would comfort her because it was so perfect.

'How is he?' Harold asked, his face pained for her and quite without that reserve that goes with suffering when it's not our own.

Blossom began to move her head and her hands in a frantic way so that her hair flicked at her face and eyes. 'I hate that place so,' she said, 'I hate the smell of it, the dirty disinfectant smell mixed up with old cooking, the lights on in the early afternoon, always on, the stairs with cigarette butts all over the place, the people, the people, how they look, all crumpled and ugly, mumbling to themselves, shouting at no one. I don't *want* him in there, I want him to come home. I don't want ever to go there again, I feel so afraid going up those stairs, smelling that smell – I can't bear it. Oh Harold, I can't bear it.'

She was now sobbing without restraint and he folded her

into his arms and rocked her a moment, then said quietly, 'But he'll be coming out soon. They said he only needed a rest, a break – he'd come to the end of his tether, that's all. It happens all the time. Please don't cry.'

'But when he comes out,' she wailed, 'it'll all be the *same* – there'll still be no work, no job, nothing, just the same. I mean, what'll he *do*?' Her voice had tipped down so low that he could barely hear it. He let her cry a little, and stroked her hair rhythmically.

Harold had gone with her once; she hadn't known the effort it had cost him to enter a mental hospital again. And he couldn't tell her. He remembered the smell, it was so nauseous, like a filthy rag thrown in your face. He'd even spoken to the doctor who said they would be trying to find Mr Bailey work – but of course, there was still, unfortunately, a stigma about being in a hospital like that. Harold, to his surprise, had snapped that there was a stigma about being out of work too.

Now he said, 'I should have gone with you, you shouldn't have to go alone.' Once Harold had had to go alone, his father had ignored the fact that his son was being admitted, as a doctor he'd decided it wasn't necessary, and that judgement made it possible for him not to visit Harold. When he came out, it was as if it hadn't happened; it was never discussed.

'He wouldn't speak to me,' she said sadly, 'he just looked ahead of him. I felt as if we'd betrayed him or something. I never realized that anyone who was so happy always could look so sad.' Her voice broke again. She righted it, 'I told him about the job you said to tell him about – he used to be good with his hands – but he didn't seem to hear me. I think he's worse than my mum says – he's terribly depressed, not just, not just a bit *miserable*.' Now she sounded angry and she was remembering that her father in his silence seemed angry too.

'You must give him time, Blossom, and you must keep on going, even if he says he doesn't want you to. I'll go with you next time, I'll wait outside with a big bunch of red roses and you can stuff your nose in them and all the smell of the place will be gone.' He took her hand and kissed it gently.

He wanted to cheer her up; he wanted her to laugh and for her face to look radiant again. He went upstairs and came down with a small, beautifully wrapped parcel which he placed in her lap. She was still downcast and listless, but she began to open it slowly, her face gradually coming to life again. Inside was a box containing some scent that she liked, but had never been able to afford.

'Oh Harold, you shouldn't have.' She opened the stopper and sniffed it. 'Oh, it's so lovely, it smells just like dolly-mixtures.' She put a little behind her ears and then hugged and kissed him. But as she replaced the bottle, her face dropped a little. It felt wrong, more wrong now, this extravagance, this spoiling of her which highlighted the deprivation she had just seen.

'It will at least get rid of the smell of the hospital,' he said, so lovingly that it hurt her.

'Harold,' she said gently, 'you mustn't give me things any more. I do love this – but it bothers me, it does really.'

He wondered if there were other reasons why it bothered her now; he felt it wasn't just the affluence – it was her reluctance to be part of him, to be in any way held by him. She had said, 'You mustn't give me things any more.' It sounded so final. So much was slipping imperceptibly into disarray. He heard another echo of it in her voice when she said, 'I can't come for the weekend, Harold, I'm sorry. We all have to take turns with the baby and the launderette and I can't really go away and leave them to do it all.' She had come to feel guilty about her own happiness, about the lazy week-ends she spent with Harold while her family worked, or went to visit her father. She felt she was letting them down, she felt they resented the easiness of her life, though her mum never said so. But her sister made cracks sometimes about her 'rich bloke down in Kensington' and sometimes she was cruel.

'That's all right,' he said, quietly, 'I understand.' But his heart had quite keeled over. The peaceful weekend routine of months was being overturned by one sentence: was she talking about just one weekend, or was everything to alter?

She was saying, 'I'm sorry, Harold, but I feel bad, you see, having a good time with you and my dad being where he is and my mum trying to manage everything. Rosina's not being much help, she's moody and angry with me because of you and she keeps taking out her own bad luck on me. I have to be there at weekends, it's the only time I can help properly.'

'The weekend's the only time you can be with me,' he said shortly. She had always kept the weekdays to herself and had come to insist more and more on this as time had gone by: 'I like to spend my nights by myself, or with Bev and the girls, or going home – I like having a life on my own.'

Was she ashamed of him? Was she refusing too close a connection, a coupling? At the beginning, she had often broken her rule. She'd ring him up on a Tuesday or Wednesday and say, 'Let's go to the pictures.' Now she never did. Now her face changed when he tried to suggest anything during the week.

Harold had become suspicious of Bev too, feeling that the friendship was subversive in some way – that Bev would set Blossom against him, that her jealousy and resentment would pinpoint his negatives. Even his generosity was coming to be turned against him because Blossom was now distinctly uneasy with it. She was listening to voices that he couldn't hear. And now the weekends were under threat, the only security he had had with Blossom was being blown apart. He couldn't let her see his fear, he couldn't let himself feel it too keenly. He began to see the instinctive wisdom in his dissembling, his hiding from her his knowledge of himself. It was right after all to have secrets from the person you loved best.

'It's all right,' he said calmly, pouring her some more tea, 'don't worry. It's just one weekend. Perhaps we can see one another one night or something? Sunday maybe?' His hand shook a little but she was blowing her nose and didn't see it.

'Yes, perhaps.' Her eyes had lost their candour, they looked into the teacup. 'Harold,' she said with a guilty pang, 'I do love you, really I do, I'm a bit confused and that, but you see, everything's changing and I must change too. I can't just go on the same with everything different.'

A vehement pain struck him so hard that he quite forgot to moderate his voice and he said loudly, 'No, Blossom, you mustn't change, *you* mustn't. Things change, life changes — your dad's depressed and your mother's frantic. But you have your own life. You can help as much as you want to, but you're not responsible for them.' He was shocked by the panic in his voice and the way his sweat ran.

'But that's just what I'm saying, Harold,' she said calmly, 'I have my own life, and my own life means I must look out for my family.'

He was stunned. She took his hand as if he was a child and said softly, 'There cannot be just you and just me, Harold, we can't hide away in this, this little house, there's the whole world outside, and it's full of dirty ugly things, and poor and rotten things. *That's* my world. This isn't.'

Now he could hear the other voices: Bev's voice, the girls' voices at the tills, over the coffee tables, the bar tables, the voices down the club, down the Hammersmith ballet classes, Rosina's voice with its ugly bitter twang, her mum's voice with its patient long-suffering tone, her dad's silent scream of disapproval. The only voice he couldn't hear was his own.

She said, 'With you it's as if nothing in the world existed, just you, just me and all these beautiful things, all that beautiful food we eat and the wine and the champagne and the flowers ...'

'And the love,' he said with a deadly smile.

'And the love,' she said, closing her eyes, 'and the love, and the love and the *love*. Harold, you're loving me to death!' Her hands flew up to her face and then nested in her hair.

A quiet despair settled over him and he was able to return to his calm and rational voice, 'Blossom, don't make the mistake of condemning me because I'm not your kind. We're all the same kind, we're all the same, we all *feel* the same things. Oh yes, we do, some of us just don't know it. Don't look for excuses to bale out on me, it's not that I'm different, or richer, or luckier; if you love me less, if you don't understand – then that's all it is. Not the other things.'

'But you never think other things count.' It was discontent looking desperately for a hook to hang on.

'They don't.'

'They *do*.'

He grew even more quiet, even more deadly as he said, 'Blossom, I understand your problems, and I even understand what you're feeling now.'

'You couldn't. You've never had them!'

Why couldn't he just tell her that he had been inside a loony bin, had smelt those smells, tasted those fears, known that slow sickness of the heart? That his sorrows, her sorrows, they were all the same. People tried to force differences to build barriers.

'You are looking for ways to leave me, Blossom,' he said sadly.

'No, I'm not.' Her voice was loud and raw. 'I must just go home this weekend, that's all.' She was sullen, and she added, 'I want to go home now.'

'Come on, then, I'll take you, my darling.'

Oh why, she wailed silently, why doesn't he tell me to stay, make me stay? But he was getting her coat.

How he pitied her her youth now; her inexperience that saw only the immediate and accessible reason; her undeveloped insight that grabbed at what she most needed and ignored the rest; that made judgements on the world and the way people lived. It was a sad pity and it showed him the distance between them; the gulf that she was so busy constructing that there was no point in him even trying to stop her.

Forty-four

When Blossom began to change a deep despair came over me. It began that first weekend she was away, and it became so acute as to remind me of the times as a child when I'd curled up into a dark cupboard, crying for the touch of my mother's hand in my hair, the lost scent of her. Her scent, having nothing to do with perfume or talc, but an animal, motherly, embracing smell. Then Blossom's scent returned to me – it was like taking the glass stopper out of an old scent bottle and being blown into the scent, then out again, and being totally possessed by the fragrance of her.

Now this scent, which entered me through my ears and eyes, through the pores of my body, was receding. I couldn't bear it. The phone never rang. I never left the house. The despair was so intolerable that I quickened it into anger – feeling that I'd let her into me entirely, opened myself to her only to see her try to scuttle away. I felt her betrayal, not only of me, but of herself, of our oneness, so keenly that I shook with rage. For just when I was beginning to regard happiness as my right, it began to escape me.

With her, I began to play the calm game that fooled everyone but me. I became inhuman again. I was good and kind, hoping that this would keep her. When she left me again, I did not complain – it was only another weekend. She had troubles, they ate into her. I told myself how unbearable it must be for her to see me working (I was still working then, in a frenzied, feverish way) and my easiness with money when she lived with the legacy of a lack of these things.

Oh, she tried very hard, she was sweet and gentle, she let me love her in my gluttonous way, but now she held back from it. I had to work harder and harder to fling her above the physical boundary into that wild abandoned state that made her shake and cry with bewilderment. And which filled me with such happiness. But then sometimes I became too passionate; my fingers pressed too hard into her flesh, my bones ground against hers so that she cried out, and that made me grind harder. Once I hurt her – she looked down and saw a livid mark on her arm and she began to disengage herself from my fingers as though they were claws. Then, I began to grow afraid too.

I was no longer Harold, no longer myself. I began to see too clearly my capacity to be wild and frightening to Blossom. I had learned from her a woman's obsession, a woman's weakness: to *live* my love affair and allow it to dominate all the areas of my life. I had become as vulnerable as a woman to the cruelties of love and had lost all the masculine detachment that makes men seem cruel. I saw that we were the same, that men and women were just the same – but women had far more courage.

But because I could still rekindle great love in her, I was saved a little longer. I went to the hospital with her the next time she went to see her father. I drove her there and parked in the car park overlooking the church with its clock that said five o'clock. She loved me that day. She had let me into the life she felt I had no place in and would not understand, she had taken me into the darkest sorrowway of it. I was going to stay outside in the car, it was what she wanted. But as she got out she turned those blue lakes of her eyes on me and said, 'Harold, come with me, please, just past that horrible rubber flapping door and to the top of the stairs. I just can't do it alone.'

I would have carried her. Kept her face against my clean shirt so those vile smells of gravy and muck and Dettol never got to her. I would have taken her poor father home and tucked him into my own bed, I would have given him a job, my job, anything, anything to bring her back to me as she had been before the rough fabric of her family life began to tear and she went with it.

And, perhaps I envied her this, this total immersion in their trouble, the closeness, the belonging they had found in adversity. I lost her through it, not because I didn't understand, or couldn't help her – but because my needs grew more colossal with her every return to them. I couldn't wait for it to lessen or pass – I panicked, calmly, rationally I panicked, and she could see my silent desperation, my casual questions yelling out their jealousy.

When she cuddled and cosseted me, I was left trembling. I lost all capacity for naturalness. No one had stroked and cuddled me before her, not in that way. Now all it reminded me of was returning home from school when I was very little to find the door open, but no one there. I was hurtling down a dangerous path and all the intelligence in the world could not save me – I knew my direction, but I couldn't alter it.

Forty-five

Bev was sitting next to Blossom at a round table in the corner of the pub. Her hair was longer now, but just as thick and glossy. With her rather stout forefinger she was drawing a daisy from a puddle of spilt beer. Without looking up she said, 'Come on, Bloss, come down the club tonight. The girls miss you.'

Blossom shook her head. Her hair was pulled back severely from her forehead in a ponytail and then plaited; her bone structure was more marked and beautifully hard.

'It'll do you good,' Bev said, then flung her hands up in exasperation. 'Honestly, it's what always happens when you're in love – you end up bleedin' miserable. Much better to go for things you can rely on, like sex.' She looked at Blossom closely, 'You having problems with that, Bloss?'

Blossom shook her head, beginning to feel angry; she kept feeling angry with Bev these days and it was nothing to do with Bev, who was just the same. Then she thought of Harold, of his body and hers, and a small shudder passed through her, something exhilarating and yet disturbing. She leaned forward and pushed her vodka away from her.

'Listen, Bev, it's nothing to *do* with Harold. I just don't want to go to the club. O.K.? I mean, I never did bloody want to go to the club anyway! I hate it.'

Bev leaned forward and shook a fag out of her cigarette case. She said firmly, 'Now look here, Blossom, this isn't about your dad, you know. I know you're upset about your dad, but it isn't about your dad.'

'Oh no?' the lovely mouth sneered.

'Oh no.' The firm cheeks of Bev took on a stony insistence. 'So what is it then, clever clogs?'

'Something's gone wrong inside you. And things aren't right between you and Harold because of it. That's why you're taking on so about your dad. Even Mrs O'Brien's noticed it, says you're not like you used to be – mooning about, forgetting things. You're not happy here any more, and you're not happy inside yourself. That's the trouble.'

'Is it then?' Blossom was nonchalant and spun her glass by the stem. Then she sat up abruptly and said, 'Look, I can't just go on seeing Harold and going to posh places and have him buying me things, I just can't, with my dad like he is. That's all.'

'What's it got to do with your dad?' Bev's square jaw moved forward with determination. 'You're not a little girl. You sound like I used to feel when I first started sleeping with blokes. I thought I was doing me dad a bad turn, that he'd be upset about it so I shouldn't do it.'

'Well?'

'Well, you can't think like that, that's all. Sometimes you sound as if your going with Harold has actually *made* your dad sick. You sort of blame him for it. It's potty.'

Blossom looked startled for a moment and quickly drank from her glass.

'Look, Bloss,' Bev touched her arm affectionately, 'I know you – and remember you've been pretty rotten to me these last few weeks too, it's as if I didn't exist, I thought you was a better friend than that. But all I'm saying is that you're carrying on strange. You've got a good fella. He's decent to you like I've never *heard* of any man being decent. He's a ruddy miracle. And there's you trying to bugger it up because of some daftness about your dad. It's *his* problem.' Blossom stiffened at the echo of Harold's words.

Bev swallowed the last of her vodka and said thoughtfully, 'But maybe you're a bit right. My mum says your dad's got worse and worse since you've been going out with Harold. That it all started, according to her, when you left home anyway.' Blossom's eyebrows flew up, and then a calm soft ripple passed across her face, a small smile tipped her lips. 'Perhaps he's beginning to feel a bit old, and then the job trouble as well. You always was his darling little girl and now you're gone. My dad was a bit funny when my sister got married. Don't worry so much about your dad, he'll get over it. He'll bounce back as long as you stay happy. You don't have to choose one or the other, you know, Bloss.' She nudged Bloss in the arm, 'Come on then, Bloss, let's have another drink and then we'll go and watch Dave's telly downstairs. O.K., Bloss?'

'O.K.,' Blossom smiled, rubbing her hand wearily across her face. Then she straightened and sat up.

'You're not as dumb as you look, Bev. And I'm sorry I've been rotten to you, I think I've been trying to blame everyone but me.' Now she looked as though she was about to cry.

'That's all right, Bloss.' Then she winked, 'You'd better watch yourself though, I might just try and get my mitts on that Harold of yours, and on that Peugeot of his as well.'

'Oh, you couldn't do that,' Blossom said sweetly, with a recharge of warmth.

'Couldn't I then?' Bev stopped in her picking up of the glasses.

'Course not. He doesn't go for girls who choose fellas by the kind of car they drive.'

'You're wrong there, darlin',' Bev said with a giggle, 'it's only the size I'm looking for.'

Blossom sat at the table; she thought of telephoning Harold. She almost got up to do it, but something stopped her. Something troubled her that she must think out first. So she stayed sitting there, waiting for something to happen. She could neither move towards it, nor avoid it. So she sat with a dark knowledge in her blue eyes. She almost whispered, as she did on long sleepless nights: something extraordinary will happen, something wonderful, just for me, something extraordinary will happen, just for me. And it's coming, I know it's coming. Oh, make it soon.

Forty-six

It was after another weekend when she couldn't come, at least not until late on Sunday night. Harold felt it was worse in a way because when she had come she'd been very loving towards him, she'd been like the old Blossom of before – only sadder. Something about her seemed to be trying to make amends and this had brought out a protective softness in him, a deep tenderness which he had not hazarded for a little while with her. His touching of her was not so much erotic as affectionate, he wanted to warm her with his body, but she was out in front somewhere, in a place he couldn't quite reach.

Now it was Tuesday. He'd visited Mrs Alexander and sorted out all her criticisms, seen Max and then gone home. But he couldn't settle to any work, and he couldn't eat although he was hungry. In the end, he found himself walking down Kensington High Street towards Marks and Spencer.

It was curious to be there now. A warm feeling still came to him as he entered the store and saw the girls in their cream dresses at the tills, but now some melancholy was attaching itself to the place and to them. He did not feel so much at home. He walked away from the main thoroughfares, among the dresses, blouses, and finally ended up at the Plant Department. He felt safer there, it was close to the Food Hall, but shaded by the tall plants. The green was so vivid it brought back the colours of Blossom's summer dresses to him. There was a fuchsia in just the shade she had worn on the beach when her skirt had whooshed up and shown her long thighs and white lace knickers. It was like swallowing something sharp to remember this now.

He couldn't see her, even though there weren't many people in the Food Hall at three in the afternoon. He was beginning to get desperate for one sight of her. It was as if here, in this shop, she was all about him – the smell of her body, her hair, the taste of her mouth, the texture of her skin – all about him, within him like a physical presence – but he couldn't see her. He felt demented. It was an absolute necessity that he see her now, this instant, even if he had to shout his head off to do so.

'Can I help you, sir?' He swung round so fast that he almost collided with the tall blonde girl who was looking expectantly at him.

'I'm sorry,' he gasped and then muttered all in a rush, 'No, no thank you. I'm just trying to decide . . .'

She smiled with that wonderfully helpful but unpushy Marks and Spencer grace. Were they taught it, or were they chosen for it? He was shaking, the girl with the immaculately made-up face was moving a little away, not to crowd him but to be there if he needed her. He could feel the sweat run down his sides. He felt quite ridiculous, and began to study the pink and mauve sprays of orchids in their sharp cellophane. He was drawn to the palest, most delicate colours and began to gather up as many of these as he could find. He began to be plagued by memories of those long lazy days lying naked in bed with her: making love when they chose, sleeping, talking, the sun streaming through the pale curtains. Blossom walking around eating grapefruit out of a tin – she preferred it to the real thing – or eating bread and jam, slice after slice. It had been as if she would never leave.

He almost ran with his handful of orchids to the cash desk.

'Can you take the cellophane off please, on all of them, I just want the flowers, in a bunch.' His voice had a harshness which he regretted, but could not control.

The tall blonde girl hesitated a moment, but then smiled and very expertly found the seam of the paper and tore it down, again and again, until all the flowers were freed. Then she arranged them carefully for him. But of course had nothing to wrap a bunch of flowers in among her pile of plastic carriers. She looked about her.

'No, no,' he moved forward, 'leave them like that, that's fine. Thank you.'

She wound a small elastic band around the stems and handed them to him with a receipt. 'Keep that, or they might stop you as you're leaving,' she grinned. 'They should be wrapped.'

'Thank you.' He was now actually shaking, and he grew furious with his body for letting him down like this.

He began to hurry towards the Food Hall, to Blossom. He rushed past the fruit and vegetables, the trifles, cream cakes, butter, cheeses, quiches – and ended up in the wine section. Where, miraculously, she was standing with her back to him, studying some papers. He stopped abruptly. How calm her back seemed in the navy-blue pinafore. It was enough just to look at her; his palpitations all subsided and he could have left then, quite easily. Normality had been returned. He was about to go when she turned.

'Harold!' It was said softly.

He stood holding his orchids, feeling the greatest pain, deep inside, tunnelling its way through his body. It ached, it ached for her.

'Are those for me?' She couldn't resist touching.

He handed them to her. For an instant she held them and pressed her face into their gleaming petals. 'I can't take them,' she whispered. She tried to make a joke, 'We're not allowed to take presents from the customers.' She touched his hand quickly, 'Harold,' she saw how his face was torn, 'take them home for me, and I'll come later, I'll come,' she repeated softly, as if for the first time she understood his desperation.

He took them and walked out of the store, numbly, his body cold and clammy at the same time. But slowly as he walked, as he remembered her promise, his senses returned; his pace quickened, his despair left him for a little.

Forty-seven

Harold had arranged the orchids in a blue glass vase which was long and round and shapely. It pleased him to see how they pressed against one another, the stems showing in a dark green mass, the blooms spilling in every direction like the curls of her hair.

Then he went back to his work. He had started it the day before; he knew what he was doing – diverting his pain and fear into something tangible. There had been many days when he couldn't even do that, when there were no words he could wrestle into shape, no solace to be found at his drawing board – when he was left with only the inescapable knot of his misery. It was primal and violent and he had to swallow it. Then he felt his aloneness most acutely and tears poured down his face. He remembered a time, on Dartmoor – when he'd been trying to pull himself out of the wreckage Rachel had left – when he had been so utterly alone, so lonely that he'd talked to a snail.

In his study he had cleared a table; it was sprinkled with flour and he had laid out some small knives and mounds of yellow stuff in lumps like clay. He was making a sculpture, he was making it out of marzipan, gently shaping it by warming it in his hands, rubbing it, moulding and forming it into the naked body of a woman. She lay on her back with her arms flung out beside her, her fingers curled, her legs apart. Her head, with its coils of hair, was tipped backwards, her eyes were closed, her lips slightly parted and smiling. He was mixing the icing sugar with water and little drops of cochineal to make a pale pink coating to cover the marzipan. The smell was quite delicious, the marzipan and icing sugar making a sweet flowery scent.

He worked carefully for hours, covering all the harsh yellow of the marzipan with the icing, letting it dry between applications. As it dried, he continued to make his delicate fruits — bunches of black and green grapes, each grape rolled separately and joined to a cluster. He made peaches, apples, plums, apricots, pears and lemons and painted each one with loving care. Then, on a peerless blue Japanese plate, he laid Blossom down, ever so gently — and all around her he arranged the fruit: a pale bunch of grapes between her thighs, peaches beside her breasts, the pears and plums making a coronet all around her.

And then, carefully, from some deep subconscious corner of himself, he found himself taking up a knife and very carefully cutting a slice out of one of the peaches. Then he laid it beside her. He knew immediately its association: the newly unearthed memory that had come back to him in Rye: his mother lying on her bed as he had last seen her. And how he had taken the peach from its plate beside her and cut with a silver knife a deep wedge of the fruit, which he had placed in his mouth and slowly swallowed. He couldn't fathom why he'd repeated it here, in this tribute and homage to Blossom; in this preserving of her beauty for a time when it might have gone from him.

When she was just as he wanted her, he applied the last coat of pink icing and let it dry. Then, with a fine brush he painted her mouth with carmine, and the nipples of her hard high breasts, the sweet little crack of her cunny, her finger and toenails. She smiled at him with her lovely Cupid's bows.

He stood back and admired her. She was a work of art, a perfect creation. She was his Blossom beautifully rendered, tenderly true to the original, preserved for ever, his for ever, most gentle in her sleep.

Forty-eight

The door clicking open downstairs startled him. He covered the sculpture and ran down the stairs. Blossom was standing at the open door with the light of the autumn evening behind her. She was wearing dark blue overalls and a green and white striped cotton shirt. It was as if the summer had returned with her. He hugged her hard, closing his eyes with relief and pleasure.

'Oi,' she said, laughing, 'stop pushing yourself up against me like that!' He realized how long it had been since she'd teased him in this way. She walked into the sitting room with an ease that suggested she felt at home; all her movements were loose again.

'Well, what shall we do tonight then, Harold?' she asked brightly, falling back into his big armchair and looking up at him.

'Why are you so happy today?' he asked carefully.

'Me dad's coming home soon,' she said with a toss of her shoulders, 'the hospital said he could come home weekend after next.'

He saw another weekend go up in smoke, but said, 'That's marvellous, what a relief.' He was actually furious with her father for causing so much distress in his life, and bitter too that his homecoming should occasion such feeling in Blossom.

'Well, we must celebrate then,' he said with a touch of irony that quite escaped Blossom.

'Oh yes, let's. Let's go for a drive in the country, it's a gorgeous evening and there won't be too many more. Let's go right now,' she said with all her old impulsiveness.

Suddenly he was happy too, ready to forgive her father, infected by her mood and more particularly by the way she had rushed up to him and thrown her arms around his neck, kissing him hotly on the mouth. He wondered whether he should show her the sculpture, but decided against it.

He drove along the M4 as she chatted about the last few days at work: Bev seeing a man stealing knickers and stuffing them into his pockets, Bev being too kind to report him; more stealing from the tills, more girls getting pregnant, in or out of wedlock; her sister being better because she'd met another fella; her mum only having to work two till six this next week. It was all as it had been – she was full of some wonderful elixir that fed into his blood only when he was close to her and poisoned him with sadness when she was gone. But it would be all right, no harm could befall them now; the gold trees in the quiet Berkshire lanes bore testimony to this.

And because she was famished and it was after eight o'clock, he wanted to feed her. He vaguely remembered someone telling him about an excellent restaurant in Bray. It tempted him, he wanted such a place to exist, some perfect place so that he could celebrate her return to him. He didn't know the area that well, and it was quite dark, but he was determined to find the restaurant and kept searching until a sign announced THE WATERSIDE INN; the name nudged his memory reassuringly and he followed the sign.

It was down a small street, close to the water, with a tall weeping willow arching over a river of swans. He made her stay in the car while he went in to check if there was a table – the idea of her being turned away would have distressed him; she must be protected from the little slights of life. But a charming Frenchwoman assured him there was room for two. He fell in love with the place, with its vases of flowers, its Victorian davenport and mellow carpets. He went to fetch her.

As they walked towards the entrance, Blossom was a little intimidated by the shiny sweep of posh cars parked outside, but he ushered her in. The Frenchwoman returned, casting a quick but eloquent glance at Blossom's informal clothing, but politely inquiring whether she had a coat, just as Blossom had caught sight of a long row of furs.

They entered a room that sloped towards curved windows overlooking the river; she could see the swans serenely gliding by in the sombre light. Ruched green and yellow curtains closed the room in with elegant intimacy. Blossom shivered a little, seeing the women were all wearing their long blacks, their ghastly taffetas bulging at the waists and arms, their fat loops of pearls.

'Bleeding hell,' she whispered, as they were escorted to a table in an inconspicuous corner, 'I feel terrible wearing these overalls with this lot.' She was blushing and sweating a little, feeling disapproving eyes on her. 'Harold, they're all staring at me,' she said with the self-conscious hurt of a child.

'If you're unhappy,' he said softly, 'we can go.'

'We *can't*!' She was appalled by the idea of getting up again, drawing attention to herself again and walking out to the accompaniment of their stares.

'Of course we can,' he repeated softly, 'just watch us.'

'No.' She grabbed his arm and hissed, 'No, we can't, it's too late.'

The waiter came with tall menus and a supercilious smile.

'Well,' Harold said, relaxing a little and reading the menu, 'the food sounds good and these rolls are home-made and delicious.'

'Why's your menu got prices on it and mine hasn't?' she demanded.

'They sometimes do that.'

'I think it's rotten, a bloody cheek,' she snapped.

'Don't let it get to you, my darling; they're French and don't know any better. Let's eat something and see if they're entitled to be so condescending.'

By now Blossom had had time to read the prices on Harold's menu. The waiter hovered, looking as though a smile would cause an internal injury.

'It's *so* expensive, Harold, how do people afford to eat in places like this? And the place is packed.'

'Expense accounts,' he said vaguely. 'Now what are you going to have?'

He had mussel soup and she had asparagus in a sauce mousseline. The second course came, and even Blossom was forced to admire the presentation of Harold's Tresse de Saumon et de Barbue au Gingembre: the two different fish cut in long strips and criss-crossed over one another in a delicate ginger sauce. But as Blossom looked forlornly at her lamb in its glossy dark sauce with a curled leaf of mint beside it, Harold felt that the evening could not be salvaged. It was toppling like a collapsed soufflé and none of his skill could prevent its fall.

Suddenly Blossom clattered down her knife and fork, her face scarlet and upset.

'What on earth is it, my darling?' Harold asked anxiously. She couldn't explain to him for a minute, she was so distressed, but eventually he learned that the chef had been making a tour of inspection to all the tables and had deliberately ignored theirs.

'He probably only goes to the people he's seen before,' Harold said sensibly.

'No, he went to everyone, everyone, except us. He did it on purpose, because of me.'

'Well, that just makes him a great fool.'

Blossom went silent, set; she felt she stood apart from the entire restaurant – because of her clothes, her background, her job, her voice and now this humiliation.

'Oh, to hell with him, Blossom, if he's such a poor judge of beauty and character, that's his loss.' But she wouldn't be comforted. And Harold felt an irrational desire to beat him up, going into his kitchen and stuffing his face into his boiling hot sauces. Not even a superb Tarte au Citron could cheer her up, and he was sad to see that she had not stolen any of the food from his plate all evening.

He drove her home, but she was silent in the car and the silence had a morose heaviness to it, as though it were filled with weighty decisions. Harold had no idea how he managed to drive the car home, because the road seemed slippery and treacherous. The trees leered over the road, closing in on him, the wheel in his hands seemed to have taken control as he drove recklessly and fast; more terrified of the moment when she would speak than he was by the idea of killing them both.

Outside his house, the car shuddered to a stop as if startled by being treated in so violent and unaccustomed a manner. Harold expected Blossom to want to go home. But she didn't. In a strange, dream-like way she walked slowly over the cobbles to his door; she turned and looked back at him and smiled an oddly tilted smile and then waited for him to let her in. He followed her and the door closed quietly behind them.

Forty-nine

It was very late. She was sitting on the throne chair and looked very beautiful; her face pale and hauntingly quiet. Her eyes, filling with the intense blue of the overalls, seemed large and tranquil in a face which, he suddenly saw, had matured and refined. Her cheeks were less full so that the bones of her jaw and cheeks sharpened her profile; and, watching her wonderful mouth, he saw again, as if for the first time, the unique quality of her perfection. He sat in the leather armchair watching her, the long mahogany table between them set with two glasses of brandy and the blue vase of orchids. They did not speak at all, and this silence was like a new sound between them, its vibrations full of dread.

He noticed that her hat was placed on the carved back of her chair. It had been lying on the back seat of his car for many weeks, but, as she got out of the car that night, she'd turned suddenly and reached for it, carrying it in. The silk poppies over the crown were startling in their redness. It bothered him that she'd taken it from his car; having it there when he drove around had been such a comfort to him. He began frantically, speechlessly, to question her motives: was she going to take it with her? Was she leaving? Would she stay with him tonight? Was she leaving? Was she leaving?

She got up without a word and walked to the window, looking out at the blackness. Her silence was becoming sinister, but he was praying that she would not end it. She left the window and walked to the hall, and then he could hear her heels tapping up the stairs. They were high heels, new shoes, and not like the shoes she normally wore, which were made of soft leather, simple and low-heeled. He realized with a shock that the shoes were rather tarty.

He could hear, by listening to her footsteps, that she'd gone into the bedroom. The cupboard opened and then closed. Then it was quiet. He was afraid to go into his own bedroom. In case she was getting her clothes together, putting them in a neat pile, looking for something to pack them in. The pink dress. A silk nightdress he had given her. The pearls. He had another brandy and waited. After a while – he charted each moment as it passed interminably slowly – he went up to her.

She was lying on top of the cream counterpane on the bed, she was asleep, lying on her back with her arms flung out and the fingers of her hands curled upwards. She was wearing the pink dress, and the luscious folds of pink satin were spread carefully about her, so that she looked like a soft blown rose with its petals wide open, about to fall. He was startled to see that her shoes were still on; somehow he wouldn't have expected this of her and it seemed a measure of her strangeness.

He went and sat quietly beside the bed, moving a chair up so he could watch her face; his hands were clasped in his lap and his face was awesome in its raw suffering. In her deep childish sleep which was so soundless, she had become like a woman he could not touch, like a statue in a chapel; she was as remote and mysterious as Mary.

After an hour she shivered and woke. It was cold and he had wanted to cover her but couldn't do it. She reached out and took his hand and a sudden, quick intimation of sorrow passed across her face. She lay still, holding his hand, and then turned to look at him.

'Harold,' she whispered, her eyes darkening, 'I feel so strange tonight, I feel so lost. I keep feeling so strange and I don't know why. When I woke up I felt that something terrible was going to happen – to me, or to you. I don't know, I don't know.' She suddenly looked down at what she was wearing, and looked puzzled, as if she couldn't remember putting it on.

He remembered her being a little like this once before; when she'd said she sometimes had premonitions. It was just before her father had had his breakdown. But her grave intensity tonight was much more marked: she was being drawn towards something that frightened her, but as the pull tautened she seemed to will it to engulf her. There was something about the way she spoke and looked that frightened him.

He decided to break the mood if he could. He took both her hands firmly in his own and said, 'Blossom, you're very tired and you've been under a great deal of strain. Tonight you found out your dad was coming home and you were wildly happy. That's often when the past strain hits you – when it's actually over. And you suddenly just flop.'

'No,' she said quietly, 'no, that's not it at all.' She rubbed her hand across her mouth. She frowned. 'That may all be true, what you said, but that's not what it is at all.'

'Have you felt like this before?'

'Before my dad, but one other time as well.'

'When?'

'It was just before my granny died. I woke up in the night and I felt some wet stuff was covering me, but there was nothing. And I knew, I just knew something was going to happen. Sometimes, at night, not so long ago, I used to think that something would happen to me, but it was a happiness, not this.'

'And this, what's this?'

'This is a sorrow.' She was quiet and very certain, as if the seed of something was already in her and she was lost to her surroundings, lost to him, already moving out of reach. She seemed drained and patient and shook her hair wearily, as if the burden of being so precious a possession would soon be lifted from her. He stared at her, he sat and stared.

Then she sat up, pulling her body backwards, lifting her left leg, the pink satin rolling lazily and lovingly down, rumpling up in a soft crush at the top of her thigh. Harold placed his hand tenderly on the swell of her thigh; he felt a slight shudder go through her.

Her face was no longer overcast; slowly, it was developing an anxious determination. He watched it as if by following its rapid fluctuations he could avoid disaster.

'Harold,' she said quietly, her hand plucking at the counterpane as his stomach knocked over his heart, 'Harold.' It was now a whisper, as if the effort of getting her words out had exhausted her. 'I need to be on me own for a bit. I'm mixed up, don't know what's happening, or what I want.' A rasping quality seemed to have crept into her voice. He was reeling a little: had she always talked with that rough accent? Had he never heard it before? Then his heart moved with pity as he saw that perhaps she had been speaking before in a more correct way just for him; perhaps she had been arranging her voice for him. Mixed up with the compassion, an insidious anger was brewing when *what* she had actually said struck him clearly.

'Meaning what?' he snapped, hearing his own voice crash, as if some heavy foot had broken a twig. And where now was that gentle voice he had reserved for her?

'Well, just that, Harold.' How strange, he thought again, had she always said his name with the letter H so muffled that it barely existed? It was difficult to keep his own voice under control with the shuddering of his body – he moved back to his chair.

'You want to go away somewhere – or do you mean you just don't want to see me again?' Now his voice was his again, just roughened, but his.

'Well, perhaps, not for a little bit.' She was arranging the folds of satin so that they covered her thighs. Some gentle impulse had compelled her to put it on that night, some softness she'd felt for him as she'd entered his bedroom. There was also a need to wipe out the ugliness of the scene in the restaurant. Now she wondered if she would ever wear the beautiful dress again.

The anguish in his face, which he was trying very hard to mask, began to hurt her and she became unkind to him because of it. Her voice reprimanded, 'I feel so sort of trapped, here; sometimes it's as if you don't want me ever to go, as if when I do I'm doing something bad to you. When I couldn't come at the weekends once or twice' – her voice was rushing headlong to get out all her thoughts and grievances of the past months – 'after that, when I came you were peculiar, I mean, you made me feel dreadful sort of, for just being with my family and not with you. I thought you were angry, you looked angry though you said nothing. And then you were, well, you were always so sort of clingy-like, so possessive and hanging on to me as if I was one of your beautiful ornaments, as if I was one of the only things you had in the world. Sometimes I felt I was being eaten alive, that there'd be nothing left of me. That you didn't want me to see Bev, or other people, not even the girls, or go to the dancing club or have a giggle with the assistant manager. Once you saw me talking to him at work, remember, and you kept asking me about him. An' he's only a stupid berk, but you went on, so quietly it drove me mad. Then I didn't want to come so much, I wanted to be on my own a bit more, I wanted to see other things, other people. And you just never did, it was just me, that's all you ever wanted. Well, it isn't healthy, it isn't. Sometimes,' her voice dropped, 'sometimes I was scared of you, really scared.'

He had to stop himself from being sick. He couldn't defend himself, he'd never argued in his life; he had to avoid a scene at all costs, he had somehow to get her to be quiet again, just quiet. Most of all he had to get this insisting voice inside him to silence its vile utterings: she's going to leave you, she's going away, she won't come back – ever, ever.

Fifty

He got up so quickly that she jumped. Her face was white and a blueness beneath her eyes seemed to infuse itself into her cheeks so that she looked cold.

Survival was such an old ally of his that he rallied, he heard himself say, 'You're right, Blossom. I have been selfish. I wanted to see you so much and I felt so alone without you. I never did before, I never felt alone until I met you. The weekends became my sanctuary, and then that first weekend was terrible, and you never rang. Oh, I'm not complaining, it's just how it was for me. When the weekends stopped happening, I panicked, I was stupid. I can see how I must have frightened you off.'

A cold shudder went through him to remember the depths of his degradation. How he had crept into the store and watched her, spied on her from various strategic positions; how he had waited in the shadows at night and watched her board the bus, how he had even followed her to see if she was really going home. How that evil god, Jealousy, had led him on, forced him to greater obediences, tumbled his pride, made him stand below her window in the hope of one glance of her – or in the wracking fear of a double shadow against the glass which was not Bev's shadow. He'd been mad, God, he'd been quite possessed. But he could end it all, start again – tonight.

He came over to the bed and sat on it, close to her, but not touching her.

'Blossom, my darling, I love you so much that I've stifled you. I'm so sorry. Don't think I haven't noticed how the fun and laughter have gone out of you. It wasn't just your family problems, it was me, blocking the light and the freedom you need. Can you forgive me? I'm a fast learner,' he laughed a quick sad laugh, 'I seem to have forgotten all the things I hold dear: I won't cramp you again, or make you feel trapped. Do whatever you want to, come when you want to, we won't get stuck again I promise. It can be just as you wish.' For a moment it even seemed to be what he wanted.

But then he saw with a steely coldness that his words had made no dent on her. He heard a silent re-run of all he had been saying and knew that all he'd been saying was, 'Don't leave me, don't leave me.' And looking at her, she was going to leave him.

Of course he had done it all wrong, he thought feverishly. She wanted him to be assertive, manly, to say, Don't go, I won't allow it. She wasn't used to his niceties, the agreeable tactics he'd used – perhaps this had been the problem all along. He was too bloody wonderful. She needed what she understood, something that made it quite clear that he wouldn't be without her. Perhaps she was even testing his resolve.

'Blossom,' he said distinctly, 'we won't talk about it any more tonight. You're tired and you must go to bed.' He moved towards her with determination.

With a wild movement, like an animal moving away from fire, she had flung herself off the bed, her heel catching for a moment in the thread of the counterpane. She grabbed at her handbag, and, if she had not done that, he might not have rushed towards her. She began to run towards the door, towards the hallway and the stairs. And he was stuck fast and couldn't move.

'Blossom!' his voice was a groan of despair that came from outside himself. 'Blossom?' He could move again, he began to run. She heard him. Her heels clattered sharply on the wood of the hallway. The clattering reached the stairs and began to descend them like falling rocks. Then a cry, a terrible cry like an animal when the claws of a trap spring around its throat. And a sound like a great heaviness, a slow motion falling, falling, falling. Then silence, utter silence.

Fifty-one

They have come. I had to let them in when the banging on my door became insupportable. In any case the time had come. I was beginning to feel like a prisoner in my own house. Besides, I feel nothing at all, so they cannot possibly hurt me.

There were two policemen. I explained to them the facts: the fall, that beautiful neck that snapped like an anemone stem. The questions began: why did I not call the police? Her mother? Her friend who was frantic with worry? Why did I wait two days? What was I trying to hide? Accidents are never hidden. And so on.

A doctor arrived. I would not go upstairs with them. I told them where to go. Then an expert of some kind came, and a man with a camera. I showed them the way upstairs. They had finished with me. I sat down here and waited again, my mind a complete blank as if acid had been poured into its cells.

When they all came down again, much later, they were different. Their faces had altered beyond recognition. They spoke to me with hatred. I heard one of them refer to me as a monster. There was something so hostile and uncomprehending about their faces it was frightening. They began to ask me more questions, one after the other, very quickly. I refused to answer them. I realized that they thought I had killed her. But it was not that that bothered them, that made them look at me as though I were a freak. After all, they had seen murderers before.

I knew I would have to speak to one of them. I chose the doctor. There was something about him that was receptive and kind. He had grey hair brushed back from his forehead and intelligent eyes. I said I would speak to him if the others left. They refused to at first, but he persuaded them.

We went into the dining room, it is the quietest room, and with all the books, it's the room I love best. I began to tell him the truth. From the beginning. I found it easy to talk. None of my emotions was functioning, it was quite easy to mouth the words and string them together coherently. We sat there a long time, he and I. He was a gentle person and I think he understood. He was a doctor quite unlike my father, who was brisk and dismissive of pain and kept rigidly to the ailments of the body. This man knew a great deal about the mind, he understood human passion. Or I believed he understood mine. Maybe I just wanted someone, one person, just to say: 'I understand, I know what compelled you.' I believe I am just like other men. He said there were a great many men and women who would understand what I had done, and why. He said there were a great many men who could have done just what I did. He helped me. Perhaps what I've always wanted, more even than to be loved, is to be understood. As you understood, Blossom, as I know you would understand now.

Of course I couldn't say too much about you, Blossom, it would have seemed irreverent. Then I sat in silence for a little while until he said, 'Tell me what you are thinking?'

And I said I could see myself as a small boy in a high walled garden, closing my eyes and calling out, Mother. And the silence. And those words in the dark chapel, *Lo, I am with you always*. And how they choked my heart like sharp thorns, like the ones on His poor head. But still there was nothing to hold, to touch, to feel, there was nothing, only that little white wafer that sometimes seemed to go dry and stick in my throat.

The doctor sits very quietly at my side, listening, thinking. He does not interrupt me or question me. Once he went down and brought me a cup of tea. As you so often did. After that I heard the policemen leave. He stayed on, he and I, for a long time. Then I began to see that there were things that he wanted to know that I wasn't telling him. Then I saw that his questions were beginning to draw me on to some deep dark place I had no strength to inhabit. And I wouldn't speak any more.

Suddenly, with no warning, a terrifying thought came to me. I got up and ran wildly upstairs to the bedroom where Blossom was. She was gone. She was gone. The bed was quite empty. My head began to spin: it was as if I saw two beds, one splattered with moonlight, with a dark bureau beside the bed and a pale blue china clock with birds on. A peach and a silver knife. And also my bed, my bed with Blossom lying quietly on it in her pink dress. And Blossom gone.

I began to scream. I was an animal clawing at the carpet – my tears and spit and the blood that had begun to seep from beneath my fingernails running together as I jerked and howled, pulling my body tighter and tighter into a knot.

Later, it could have been hours or minutes, but later I saw someone standing in the room. The doctor. He didn't move towards me. He simply waited. And when my body finally subsided, I saw him come and kneel beside me. I noticed with a shock that there were tears in his eyes. I noticed also an expression on his face that I could read: it was relief. He touched my arm, with tenderness, I thought.

But I was feeling and seeing again, and he knew that I couldn't bear it. I allowed him to give me the injection.

Fifty-two

From the way that Blossom lay at the foot of the stairs, with her neck buckled against the wall, and her body foetally curved into her long pale legs, Harold knew. Knew it in the only way he could – logically and intellectually, because death was not something he had ever faced, it was a word he shied away from even on paper.

Now, as Blossom's body lay at his feet, he bent down and very tenderly moved her head so that it shouldn't lie at such an uncomfortable, twisted angle. It seemed to him that her body had not toppled and crashed to the bottom of the stairs at all – but, by the grace of her limbs and the sweetness of her flesh, had merely been poured quite gently down. And then stopped.

He knelt down and kissed her. A memory returned of how his mother had always come up to his room and kissed him good-night, bending over him with her face like a sacrament that would remain with him all night. He rested his face against Blossom's and waited for a while, his mouth close to hers, as if he expected that lovely voice, so full of emotion, to suddenly bubble again and call to him. As if she would suddenly turn her head and spring kisses at him – as if she had teased him quite enough.

He sat there with her for an hour or so; it was getting cold and the light shining down from the hallway above them seemed harsh and bright. He shaded her eyes from it. Her head was cradled in his lap and with very slow, dream-like strokes he brushed her hair away from her cool cheeks. But she was getting colder. So very carefully he tried to lift her.

As he did so, he noticed that the whole of the left side of her face had turned a livid purple; it had swollen with bruising, distorting her face, making the creamy skin of her other cheek painfully perfect and unflawed. The pain of this crumpled him for a moment, and he wept, turning his face away. But then, he looked at her again and the sight of her like this – her flesh broken and bruised, her beauty vanished – was the most profound experience of his life. The most profound pain and the most profound experience of love. In that moment, his love was distilled; it became quite pure. It was as if love had blown every other emotion clean out of his body and he had become transported by the deepest feeling it is possible to feel.

He carried her up the stairs, drawing her body close to his; he held her like a child who needs the closest connection with a comforting body when it's in pain; he didn't feel the weight of her. He walked very slowly, like a man wading through waves, and every now and then he stopped to lovingly brush his lips against hers. He carried her to his bed, brushed her hair, and covered her gently. Then he undressed and got into bed beside her.

All night long he lay beside her body; sometimes the chill of her made him feel he was being turned to stone. All was suspended in him: all thought, all sensation. He moved his hands constantly over her body, trying to stoke some small spark of warmth in her limbs. Then he lay still, just holding her against him, hour after hour. The longest hours of the night passed and still he held her, still he could not let her go, he pulled her closer against his side and rocked her.

As the night came to an end, a delirium crept into him, a raging fever that made him shiver violently. He burned, his flesh burned as if some wild hope of the mind tried in this way to rekindle her, to recharge her veins and make her heart beat again. He felt his body crackle with the heat so much that he felt she must catch fire. But, in the end, it was her temperature that melted him.

By dawn great banks of slow-moving clouds reflected the first glow of morning, birds sang in his garden and there was a sharp clear light flooding the bedroom. When he looked at

Blossom with her uncoiled hair, her face had a fragile, piercing loveliness that no bruising could mar. She seemed to sleep in innocence. He looked around the room with a sad perplexity: he had woken after that long terrible night expecting everything to have changed. It was impossible that the world inside and outside the room they lay in was unaltered. But it was.

He turned back to Blossom and uncovered her gently. Waves of loud, resounding shock assaulted him again. Seeing her body rigid in the pink dress, her face with its ghostly pallor, flung him quite out of his mind to a place far, far beyond. He was a child again, with a six-year-old heart torn apart by disbelief and grief so great that it couldn't be endured. A scream began in his throat, but it didn't reach the air outside, it was trapped there.

Fifty-three

I cannot remember the day that followed that night. I feel now as if I did not move at all from that bed where I lay holding her. For hours nothing seemed to happen, but sometimes I fell into such deep reveries that it's possible I might have slept or dreamt. And then there was the night again. A night of complete and terrible madness.

There was a feeling all that night of her coming and going. I listened for a key turning in a lock, a touch returned, a shadow against a wall, a shape somewhere against a curtain, the return of a presence, her presence, a scent in the air, the fragrance of her body. Sometimes I seemed to hear her voice whispering to me, an eerie fluttering sound that beckoned to me from the corners of the room. But the whispering and the feeling of her presence coming and going comforted me. I knew she hadn't left me. She hadn't gone to that unreachable place where I would not find her again.

I left her for a short while and went downstairs. My head felt so strange, it was full of images that paralysed me. I drank some brandy and sat in my chair. Then I saw her hat: I felt as though I had been cut in two. It seemed to me that death had come to all my things, my furniture lay heavy and silent. I had as little consciousness as the objects in that room and everything around me had become quite unreal.

But then again she came to me. I felt her close to me, at my elbow, in the crook of my arm, it even seemed to me that she curled up in my lap, gave a little sigh and fell asleep.

Then I saw her, moving slowly, softly, by the window. She was letting go, she was going, receding into the darkness, walking backwards from me, her long white arms held out as if she implored me to keep her, to hold her back. She was smiling at me, beckoning me to come with her. But when I moved to follow, her hands rose up to restrain me – she wasn't beckoning me, she was asking me to save her, to take her back, to keep her from that dark airless place.

Oh Blossom, I went totally and hideously insane; the unendurable was happening, your spirit was leaving me, would leave me for ever. Everything went black and silent. I was streaming with tears. I knew that I was losing the source of my only joy and would never again feel the love, joy, peace that lived and breathed only in you. I was being torn from you, limb from limb, flesh from flesh.

I turned to run away – but I couldn't leave you, oh Blossom, how could I leave you? So I turned back. And saw that you had gone.

I ran towards the light by the window, but my body fell straight through it. I turned away in horror.

Then I caught sight of my face in the mirror, in the mirror where you used to smile at yourself, and I saw that my hair had gone white.

Fifty-four

He walked upstairs, shivering violently. He walked like an old man and sometimes he seemed to stagger. Time had become stretched out of shape, he had no idea how many days and nights had passed, or when he had last slept or eaten. His vision and his feelings were peculiarly intense.

He walked very slowly into the bedroom, and with the greatest difficulty raised his eyes to the bed. She lay there still. She was still there. He ran up to her and buried his face in her hair with exhausted relief and began to sob quietly, rocking both their bodies tenderly.

As he lay beside her, a great calm came to him; a washed-up feeling of near collapse. He knew that only her body could save him. Her body was the bridge between him and the void – her body within him, part of him. Her body becoming his as a final marriage between them. He would join them in a sacred act which would grant him her powers of protection and love in her absence.

Her words returned to him, as clear as they had been on that bright afternoon as she lay on the grass looking up at him, and said: 'Yes, I would eat you, to keep me from dying . . .'

Fifty-five

Harold sat alone at the dining-room table in his red brocade chair. In the centre of the table was the blue vase of orchids, just as beautiful and fragrant as when he had bought them. How long ago that seemed. The room was lit by long white candles in tall candlesticks. The flickering light lit up the glossy spines of the books along one wall and drew out the molten colours in the mirror. His glass was filled with claret, and he turned the cut-glass decanter slowly to catch the iridescent lights. The thin porcelain plate in front of him had a sheen like a luxurious fabric and the silver was ornate and old-fashioned. Set out beside him was a small covered dish, and beside that, a Victorian spoon inlaid with an enamelled pink rose.

He closed his eyes for a moment, his hands digging into his white hair. He was remembering how she had stood in the pink dress, just over there, looking at herself in the mirror. And how he'd come up behind her and kissed her. And how she'd sprung at him like a cat and bit him below his jaw, hard, deep, so that the blood ran. She had loved him, oh how she had loved him. With such a fierce passion, such heated urgency in her wanting him.

His face had a curious wonder, like a man who has made a long, lonely pilgrimage and reached at last the feet of his saint. He sat very still, his face radiant with that pure love that had first come to him when he'd seen Blossom's broken face; he was in the same state of grace. Soon he would be more so.

MORE ABOUT PENGUINS, PELICANS AND PUFFINS

For further information about books available from Penguins please write to Dept EP, Penguin Books Ltd, Harmondsworth, Middlesex UB7 0DA.

In the U.S.A.: For a complete list of books available from Penguins in the United States write to Dept DG, Penguin Books, 299 Murray Hill Parkway, East Rutherford, New Jersey 07073.

In Canada: For a complete list of books available from Penguins in Canada write to Penguin Books Canada Ltd, 2801 John Street, Markham, Ontario L3R 1B4.

In Australia: For a complete list of books available from Penguins in Australia write to the Marketing department, Penguin Books Australia Ltd, P.O. Box 257, Ringwood, Victoria 3134.

In New Zealand: For a complete list of books available from Penguins in New Zealand write to the Marketing Department, Penguin Books (N.Z.) Ltd, P.O. Box 4019, Auckland 10.

In India: For a complete list of books available from Penguins in India write to Penguin Overseas Ltd, 706 Eros Apartments, 56 Nehur Place, New Delhi 110019.